SILENCE
OF THE
NINE
T. STYLES
NATIONAL BEST SELLING AUTHOR OF *RAUNCHY*

Are You On Our Email List?

PUBLISHER'S NOTE:
This book is a work of fiction. Names, characters, businesses, Organizations, places, events and incidents are the product of the Author's imagination or are used fictionally. Any resemblance of Actual persons, living or dead, events, or locales are entirely coincidental.

Library of Congress Control Number: 2014935067
ISBN 10: 0989084582
ISBN 13: 978-0989084581

Cover Design: Davida Baldwin www.oddballdsgn.com
www.thecartelpublications.com
First Edition
Printed in the United States of America

Library of Congress Cataloging-in-Publication Data

Styles, Toy, 1974-
Silence of the nine / by T. Styles.
pages cm
ISBN 978-0-9890845-8-1 (pbk. : alk. paper)
1. Criminals--Fiction. 2. Children of criminals--Fiction. 3. Family secrets--Fiction. 4. Daughters--Fiction. 5. Drug abuse and crime--Fiction. 6. Incest--Fiction. 7. Urban fiction 8. Psychological fiction. I. Title.
PS3619.T95S55 2014
813'.6--dc23

2014009493

What's Up Fam,

Man, I'm writing this letter after being up all night reading the novel on deck, "Silence of The Nine". This fucking book had me in awe. The story is so fresh, exciting, disgusting and at the same time, regal. T. Styles's creativity is unmatched in this game and I know you will fall in love with her latest work, just as I have. Prepare yourself.

Keeping in line with tradition, we want to give respect to a vet or trailblazer paving the way. With that said we would like to recognize:

Tracy Br wn

Tracy Brown is the veteran author of classic novels like, "Black"; "White Lines 1 and 2"; "Twisted"; "Snapped" and "Aftermath". Tracy has been in this game for over a decade and will continue to make her mark in the industry. The Cartel Publications supports her work completely. Make sure you do the same and check her out.

Aight, go ahead and dive in! I'll get at you in the next novel.

Be Easy!
Charisse "C. Wash" Washington
Vice President
The Cartel Publications
www.thecartelpublications.com
www.facebook.com/publishercwash

Instagram: publishercwash
www.twitter.com/cartelbooks
www.facebook.com/cartelpublications
Follow us on Instagram: Cartelpublications

ACKNOWLEDGMENTS

I acknowledge every reader who continues to purchase my novels. You and I have a strange love affair. We are brave enough to submerge ourselves into a story instead of spectating from the outside.

DEDICATION

I dedicate this novel to my love. You have always completed me.

Of all base passions, fear is most accurs'd.

- ***William Shakespeare***

PRESENT DAY

WINTER, BALTIMORE, MD

PENN STATION

The snowstorm was unmerciful as the train conductor yelled, "All aboard! All aboard!"

When Amtrak's train doors opened a beautiful woman bombarded her way past passengers as she rushed toward the center of the railcar. A newborn baby, not even three days old, was nestled against her breasts and was dangerously close to being smothered.

Frantically she pushed past customers who looked at her angrily as she knocked them over in an effort to get as far from where she entered as possible. As she made her way deeper into the rail car, she avoided a coach seat and elected to sit in the dining car area instead. It was booth style seating and a cream table sat in the middle.

The woman scanned her surroundings and when she didn't see anyone coming she exhaled and took a seat. Breathing as if she just ran a 5K marathon, she removed the baby from her chest and he howled in an attempt to breathe. She hadn't meant to suffocate him but they were running for their lives.

Relieved that they were both alive and unharmed, she looked at the child. He was perfect. In every way.

Wanting to quiet him down, she ran her index finger over the baby's vanilla colored cheek and a tear fell from her eye and dripped on his upper lip. He simmered down as he looked into the woman's eyes. She loved the little boy. More than another human could. She wanted nothing more than to take care of him and give him the life he deserved. But there was one problem. She was uncertain about her future.

There was no use in harping on what was to come. She would have to deal with shit as it flew her way. So she placed the sheet under the baby's neck to be sure he was warm. This winter was brutal and at first she was afraid that her train would be cancelled but for now she was lucky. And she hoped her streak would continue.

When the baby was cozy, she took one more look around. When she was certain that the car she was in was empty she leaned her head against the cool window. Glancing outside, she exhaled at the snow falling out of the heavens and covering everything in sight. Baltimore looked festive. If only she were in the holiday spirit.

Since she had been running for her life she hadn't slept in two days. So when the train began to move, she decided now was as good a time as any. Exhausted, she dosed off and when she awoke she was staring at the Predator who haunted her dreams.

Although the Predator was deadly, she looked regal sitting across from her. The chocolate fur coat she donned brushed against her high cheekbones and her eyes seemed to pierce the frightened woman's soul.

Two men, that the woman was certain were armed, stood behind the Predator while she remained as cool as an icicle. “Hello Butterfly,” the Predator said smoothly, “now did you really think you would get very far?”

“I…I’m so sorry. It’s just that I—”

The Predator raised her hand silencing the woman instantly. “Butterfly, I don’t want to hear your lies,” she said with a smile. “I’m tired. I’m very, very tired. You put me through a lot to catch you.” She looked down at the sleeping baby in her arms. “And judging by the redness of your eyes you must be too.” The Predator leaned in and observed the baby. “Aw…he’s beautiful isn’t he?”

Butterfly sobbed louder, in the hope that someone would hear her and ask what was wrong. “I’m so sorry for what I did. It was before I knew I was three months pregnant. Please don’t hurt me.”

“There’s no use in trying to gain an audience. Six of my men are outside of this cart and they won’t let anyone come in. So save your energy, Butterfly. Besides this meeting is long overdue.”

“What are you going to do to me?”

“Nothing you don’t deserve. That you can believe.”

Butterfly had a feeling that nothing she said would keep her safe. The performance she was giving was unsolicited and the Predator wasn’t interested so she tried to calm down. Emboldened by the reality of her situation she said, “You’re evil. Just plain old evil.”

“You call me evil?” The Predator questioned. “After what you’ve done to me.”

“I know you. And you’re far more evil than me. Just like Kerrick.”

PART ONE

CHAPTER ONE
KERRICK
FEBRUARY 1966

SAKUBVA, MUTARE - SOUTH AFRICA

"I'll note you in my book of memory."
-William Shakespeare

The afternoon heat was unforgiving as Kerrick Khumalo pressed his dick deeper into the pinkness of his wife's warm pussy. He lay on his back in their sweltering bedroom as Thandi switched her hips back and forth on top of him like she was driving a stick shift. She was a spectacle to behold. One of the Wonders of the World. In his entire life he had never met anyone like her, and he doubted he ever would again.

She was so wet that her syrup poured over his dick and dampened the sheet beneath his body. He ran his hands over her bistre colored skin and admired the darkness of her tone against his ebony complexion. They looked picture perfect together. Harmonious.

As the pleasurable sensation overcame her Thandi looked down at him and in her native language proclaimed, "Fuck me, Kerrick. Make me your whore."

He adored when she talked dirty because it wasn't in her character. Both of her parents were farmers and devout Christians. To even marry her took work and a promise to protect her always was necessary. In order to gain her hand in marriage Kerrick had to give her parents two goats. But he would've given them five if he could've married her all over again.

He didn't always feel the need to be faithful. At sixteen years old, before Kerrick even thought about marriage, he was a player. He would promise marriage to virgin women and once they gave him their hearts and bodies, he would start vicious rumors about them being whores throughout the village. That way he would have an excuse on why he'd call the marriage off. But Thandi was different. He wanted her.

She was also a virgin, which meant her pussy was already tight. But at seventeen, as a gift to Kerrick, her parents made her undergo painful vaginoplasty to tighten it even more. This, they felt, would secure a long marriage and make her husband happy.

Surgeons cut into the walls of her vagina and tightened it up with stitches, so sex would be more pleasurable for Kerrick. She was lucky to still have her clitoris because originally her parents suggested that the doctor's remove it too. So that she wouldn't desire another man. But Kerrick said that was unnecessary because he wanted his wife to enjoy their time together.

Thandi continued to buck her hips wildly and when she felt herself about to cum, she rose up a little and slammed back onto him, like a hammer hitting a nail. Kerrick always enjoyed that movement because it forced him to ejaculate quickly. And this time was no different.

When he felt her body tremble he shoved deeper into her mound and splashed his semen inside of her.

Thandi collapsed on top of him and placed her head on his hairy chest. Her short cotton-like bush brushed against his nostrils and smelled of sweet sweat. He inhaled deeply. There wasn't a thing about her he didn't adore. She was his world. His soul. And the only thing or person who drew breath that he cared about.

As Kerrick tried to come down from his sexual high he considered his life. Things were looking up for him and his beautiful wife. In Africa he attended the University of Zimbabwe and at eighteen years old, he was awarded a Visa to attend John Hopkins University on an engineering scholarship in Baltimore Maryland. Since he was allowed to take his wife, this meant that both of them would have a chance at a better future.

America was the place where dreams came true. He studied the customs so intensely that although he had an accent, he sounded more American than anybody in his village. He worshipped the country and was certain they were going to love him when he finally arrived.

"I love you, Thandi," he said as he rubbed her damp hair and looked down into her eyes.

"I know, my dear husband," she continued trying to regain her breath.

"There is nothing I wouldn't do for you."

She wiggled on top of him and he could feel the rush from her heated pussy. "I know, my dear husband."

Suddenly he gripped a fist full of her hair and yanked backwards. Forcing her to look into his eyes. "And if you ever left me I would kill you."

Although her scalp stung from hairs being snatched out by his power, she wrestled from out of his grasp, straddled him and slapped him in the face repeatedly until her palm burned. When she was done inflicting pain on him, which he loved, she lowered her head and kissed him softly on his bottom lip before biting it so hard it bled.

"And I would do so many things to you, if you ever left me, or didn't keep your vow to protect me." She released his lip and blood trickled from the wound and trailed toward his chin. "Including come back in a later life and kill you." She licked the blood off before giggling.

Kerrick's dick stiffened again and he smiled. This was the other reason he loved Thandi. Although her virtue was in tact before they were married, she held violent tendencies. Just like him.

Unlike the other women he dated in high school, who allowed him to sleep around with other women, including their friends, Thandi would attack him in public and dare him to fuck another if he wanted to keep his dick. He wore a raised stab wound to his lower back to prove it. Thandi was a firecracker and that made her all the more appealing and vicious.

When the phone rang she rolled off of him and crawled toward it on the table by the bed. She plopped down on her belly, and her tight ass cheeks sat up in the air like two firm melons. Because she was on her stomach and her legs were slightly open, her pink pussy stood out against her chocolate skin and had him wanting to dig into her all over again.

"Hello," she said, popping her ass cheeks like the girls in the American porno movies, knowing that her young husband was watching. "Oh, Afua," she said cheerfully. "My dearest friend. How are you?"

"I'm fine. This baby is keeping me up all hours of the night of course. But how are you?"

"Great. Just preparing to leave for America," she said proudly.

"I know, my friend," she sighed. "That's what I wanted to talk to you about. When do you think you could come over, Thandi? I'd like to prepare a meal for you before you leave. You know…how we use to do years ago."

Afua and Thandi had been friends since they were toddlers. When Kerrick first met Thandi, Afua was with her. At first he was attracted to them both but it was Thandi's sharp tongue and witty conversation that won him over. He'd been pleased with his decision ever since.

But Afua wasn't a slouch and therefore she wasn't single for long. After awhile she married Ulan and they had a beautiful baby together. Although Ulan didn't have the intelligence to go to college like Kerrick, he was a workingman and provided for his wife and six month old baby the best he could. In the fields.

"How about tonight?" Thandi said. "I can make some hibiscus punch and we can chat for hours." She giggled.

"Oh no," Afua said in a disappointed tone. "To-night would usually be great but Ulan is not here. And I won't have anyone to care for the baby. Besides, he wanted to say goodbye to you also."

Thandi rolled on her back and looked at her husband who was eyeing her as if she were a piece of steak. She widened her brown thighs to give him a greater view. Her pussy opened like a rosebud and whispered his name.

Turned on, Kerrick crawled on top of her and stuck his dick into her warmth as she continued her conversation. Her body shivered with delight.

Damn I love this man. She thought.

"On second thought tonight won't be good for me either," Thandi said as Kerrick moved inside of her. "My husband gets off early tonight and he wants to take me out to dinner before we leave for America. Tomorrow he works all day and that will be better for me."

"Oh…I…I want to see you sooner than that. It's urgent."

Thandi sensed something in her friend's voice and Kerrick sensed something wrong with his wife. Thandi's body tensed up and he looked at her with concern. "Why do you sound unhappy, friend?" Thandi asked.

"It's just that I want to tell you something but I'm not sure if I should. It may not be my place."

"What is it about?"

"Kerrick," she said firmly.

Thandi's eyes squinted. "What about Kerrick could have you so unhappy?" she giggled.

Kerrick pulled out of his wife and looked down at her. Now he was concerned since he was a part of the conversation.

"I've been hearing things," she swallowed. "Awful things and I want to talk to you about them first. But let me not ruin the day. Tomorrow works for me, Thandi. What time can you come over?"

"I'll be there at noon. But is there something I should be concerned about?"

"That's up to you. I'll see you tomorrow."

When she hung up Kerrick looked at her with an accusatory stare. "What's going on?" he asked. "Why are you upset?"

"That was Afua. She said she wanted to talk to me about something."

He bent down and kissed her chin. "About what?"

"You."

He rose up and laughed. "What could she possibly want to say about me?" He got out of bed and slipped into his black slacks on the floor. "The woman doesn't even know me."

He watered his plants, a hobby that was handed down to him by his mother before he had to kill his parents to avoid being tortured by Chimwanje, a militant group trained by the guerillas. Kerrick was taken by the same group and tossed from village member to village member, where he was raped by men and sold to others for profit and slavery. When asked why he was raped and not allowed to fight for the rebel they said he was too soft. And only the most violent ruled.

"Are you sure you are being faithful?" she asked him honestly.

Kerrick ambled over to the wooden chair in the room and slipped into the white t-shirt he wore earlier. "Thandi, I'm going to pretend that you didn't just ask me that."

Her disposition seemed serious. "Are you fateful?" Unlike some women, she did not fear him.

He sat on the edge of the bed and placed on his brown loafers, no socks. He also slid the red ribbon bracelet that Thandi made him in art class on his wrist. "You already know the answer to that."

"And yet you ignore my question anyway."

His brows lowered. "Never forget that a lot of women in this village are envious of you," he responded. "We are going to have the life together that they always dreamed of. Don't get replaced because you don't trust me." He stood up and walked toward the door. "There are plenty of you my beautiful, Thandi. But there is only one of me."

The nighttime fell on Zimbabwe bringing with it a warm breeze. The darkness acted as cover as Kerrick approached the shack with vengeance in his heart. Before breaking into the house he looked behind himself and then removed a knife from his back pocket. Carefully he stuck the blade into the keyhole of the door and it popped. Once he turned the handle slightly it clicked.

He had gained entrance.

Kerrick pushed the door open and crept inside slowly. The floor creaked under the pressure of his weight as he eased toward the back bedroom. He arrived at a wooden door, which was welted due to Africa's sweltering heat. He approached the door and placed his ear against the paneling. From inside he heard heavy breathing. The door creaked when he entered and the snoring ceased.

Startled, Afua sat straight up in the bed when she realized she was not alone. She pushed back into the headboard and brought her legs against her chest. Her face glistened due to the moonlight shining against the sheen of sweat covering her chocolate skin. "I knew you would be coming." Her tone was calm but she was horrified. Her eyes darted around her room and landed on the machete her husband used to cut sugar cane on the floor next to the door. She considered running for it.

"You'll never make it," he warned. "I'm quicker and more deadly. Tell me, Afua. How did you know I would come tonight?" he took one step inside.

"I dreamed of you."

He raised the knife in his hand and rubbed the tip. It pricked his fingertip. He had been around violence so much that he loved murder. "Why did you have to stick your nose into my business, Afua? I would've never acted so hasty had you not violated my marriage. Don't you realize how much I love my wife? And how far I will go to protect her from my secrets?"

"I wasn't thinking, Kerrick. I love my friend truly." A single tear rolled down her face and dampened her white cotton bra. "I always have and always will. And I thought she should know that you steal babies for profit."

"That's your biggest problem. You think your love trumps mine," he bellowed. "She is my wife and I will go to the ends of the earth to keep her impression of me pure!"

Afua exhaled. It was as if all of the air was pressed from her body. She knew there was nothing she could say to him. Her time in this life had expired. "Before you kill me," her body trembled as she reconciled with her fate, "I need to know something. About my son, are you going to sell him too?"

"That's no longer your worry."

Her forehead crinkled. Now she was enraged. "If you take my son everything you touch will be cursed. Your food. Your children and even your wife's lovely face."

Enraged that she threatened him Kerrick stepped in further and crawled on top of the bed. Afua tried to run but he overpowered her and straddled her body. He felt superior as he stared down at her. His eyes squinting as rage coursed through his blood. "Afua, you must not ask the questions to the things you don't want to know."

Tiring of her, he slammed the blade into her throat and her eyes popped open. Blood splattered on his eyelids and his mouth. When he was sure she was dead, he crept to the room where her baby lie in the crib. He looked down at the child and watched it sleeping peacefully.

The more children he stole from their mothers, the more heartless he had become. He wanted to see if he would spare Afua's husband's only child. But for one thousand dollars he decided he couldn't. So he removed the baby from the crib and washed into the night.

Kerrick ambled five miles on foot until he arrived at his destination. The child cried a few times but for the most part, he remained silently sleeping. Needing some rest, he approached the bench and waited for his customer.

The child cooed and tossed but Kerrick never looked directly into its face. He didn't want the child's features etched in his memory. This type of work was heartless and it took a man like Kerrick, one who was both ambitious and selfish to do the job. His cold manner made him a pro.

Thirty minutes later a late model blue ford pickup pulled up in front of Kerrick. A cloud of dust twirled into the wind. Kerrick stood up and greeted him with a nod of the head. The child was firmly in his arms.

Ochi, a man who led a sex driven lifestyle, hopped out of the vehicle and walked over toward him. "Is this the child?"

Kerrick nodded and handed him the baby. Ochi reached into his pocket and handed him five hundred dollars. Kerrick counted each bill in front of him.

"It took you long enough," Ochi said, hoping to break Kerrick off of his count.

"You're short," Kerrick exclaimed, still examining the bills. "Where's the rest of my money?"

"Are you sure?" Ochi said. "I just counted it and it was all there."

Kerrick threw him a glare. A deadly one.

Ochi knew if he persisted in lying to Kerrick, he would meet his demise. So he stuffed his hand into his pocket and grabbed five crumpled one hundred dollar bills. He slapped it into his hand and scowled. "Here. Take your money, baby napper!"

Kerrick counted the cash again and this time he was correct. So he folded it and placed it into his pocket.

"Why did it take you so long?"

"It doesn't matter how long it took me. You're still HIV positive right?" Kerrick walked away without waiting on an answer. "That's all you should be worrying about."

Ochi watched him as he walked up the dirt road and faded out of sight.

Kerrick had a deadly job and he owned up to it. Africa had one of the highest HIV rates in the world and Kerrick capitalized on it. He, and many others, believed in the Virgin Cleansing myth. In their warped minds they believed that if they had sex with a virgin child, preferably a baby, they would be free of HIV. To the date Kerrick had stolen over twenty babies in an effort to raise enough money to have a good start in America. He was as evil as they came.

This awful line of work was the reason he had to kill his wife's best friend. Afua caught on to what he was doing and was going to let Thandi know, and Kerrick decided to stop her the only way he knew how. Through cold blooded murder.

The night sky continued to spread over Africa like a blanket. Sweat poured down Kerrick's back and several mosquitoes took to chewing on his flesh. After delivering the baby to his customer, Kerrick walked five blocks to the Chaka Bar. He was due home an hour ago but his line of work always made it difficult for him to sleep. And there was only one thing that could cure his ailing heart. Liquor. And plenty of it.

Kerrick strolled up to the makeshift bar and grabbed a plastic white chair. It scraped along the dusty ground as he pulled it to a table. Trying to prevent sweat from pouring down his eyes he grabbed a napkin off of the table, wiped his brow and flagged over a sexy African native with an ass as high as a basketball hoop and as tight as a guitar string. She was an example of why Africa had some of the most beautiful women in the world.

The delightful waitress smiled when Kerrick caught her attention, and grabbed a pencil and pad off the bar. She sashayed in his direction more than ready to take his order. The red shirt she wore barely covered her miniscule breasts and her white shorts clutched her ass like shackles to a death row inmate.

"How can I help you?" she asked smiling widely. Kerrick was a regular customer and she knew the drunker he was the better the tip.

"The usual."

She licked the lead at the tip of the pencil and said, "Vodka and brandy coming up." She wrote down his order and went to fulfill it.

As he waited he glanced over at a group of women dancing in a herd. There bodies glistened under the leaning lamp, as the base from the speakers possessed their moves. Life in Africa, one of the poorest countries in the world, always seemed brighter when music filled the air.

All of the women put on a performance for Kerrick. They were sexy no doubt but not one of them could hold a candle to his beautiful wife Thandi. And he would give anything, including his life, and the life of innocent babies, to make her happy.

A half hour later Kerrick was on his second drink. The plan was to stop where he was but his mind was on Afua. He had killed many in his lifetime. So many he could no longer maintain count. But the curse she stuck on him had him worried for his future and he didn't know how to shake it. He hadn't known Afua to deal with black magic, but with the confident way she cursed him, he couldn't be sure.

As he nursed his second drink he eyed the women and their show. Every time they bucked their hips, they looked in his direction to make sure that he was watching. He had no intentions of fucking any of them but since he just killed his wife's best friend and sold off her baby for profit, he could use the mental escape.

"So you're the reason I can't get their attention," An American said standing behind Kerrick.

When Kerrick turned around he was staring up at a tall white man with eyes as green as the Caribbean sea. "May I have a seat?"

Kerrick shrugged and lifted his half empty cup, "It is a public place." He turned back around and focused on the women.

Although Kerrick's disposition screamed calm, his heart thumped around in the trunk of his body and he felt uneasy. He doubted that a white American would busy himself with a half a dozen missing African babies but he couldn't be sure. America was known for butting in other countries business.

"I'll take that as a yes." The strange gentleman flopped down clutching a half drunken beer in his hand. He leaned back in his seat, which squeaked. "I can't believe I'm in Africa," he moaned before taking a large gulp of beer and slamming it down on the table. "Young man, I see your cup is almost empty. Want another?"

Kerrick shrugged. "I guess so."

The stranger waved the bartender over and she brought the stranger another beer and Kerrick another drink.

"I'm Peter Cramer by the way," he said extending his hand. The tips of his fingertips were as red as cherries. "And you are?"

"Kerrick Khumalo." Kerrick shook his hand.

"So I take it this is your native country," the stranger asked.

"I've lived here for most of my life. But next week my home will be in Baltimore Maryland in America."

Peter's eyes widened. He appeared overly excited as he moved around in his seat. "Are you serious?"

"Very."

"Tell me. What brings you there?"

"I have obtained a Visa for school at John Hopkins University. Me and my lovely wife of course. And I'm looking forward to a beautiful future together in the land where dreams come true. In fact I've earned it."

"Well isn't this something," he nodded. His eyes were on Kerrick but he appeared to be looking through him and not at him. "I'm from America too. And I am here to spearhead a new project for my company. Cramer Construction and Associates also in Baltimore." He took another gulp. "We're building luxury buildings here, in the hopes of stimulating the economy." He boasted. "So what is your major?"

"I'm an engineer."

The stranger leaned in. "You can't be serious," he proclaimed, afterwards slapping the table almost spilling both drinks.

"I am very serious," Kerrick smiled as he started to appreciate the gentleman's vigor for life.

The stranger reached into his pocket, grabbed a small silver case and removed a red and black card. Now Kerrick didn't feel so uneasy since he was certain the man was not there for him. "Take this and when you reach America, contact me. We're always looking for engineers."

Kerrick looked down at the card with hopeful eyes. He always worried about the next step after he secured a degree. Could the strange man with the cherry fingertips be the answer? "Should I wait until after I attain my degree to contact you?"

"Heck no," he chuckled jovially. "I'd like you to contact me the moment you touch down. We need good interns we can teach you the business too."

Kerrick's smile was so wide he felt clownish. It was unlike him to get wound up by hopes and dreams. He was a man of action and realized that in life things didn't always go his way. "I will contact you, sir," he smiled widely while nodding his head. "I most certainly will."

The stranger leaned back again and looked over at the women in a huddle. They looked like snakes being charmed by a Pungi instrument. Back home he would watch black women from a far, admire their thick bodies and chocolate skin before beating his dick in the bathroom at work. But in Africa, he could indulge. He could satisfy all of his desires.

"Look at those women," Peter said to himself. "I have done all I could to win their attention but they don't seem to be interested in me. Maybe my pale skin and large personality is too much for them," he said arrogantly.

"Which women?" Kerrick asked. He had forgotten all about the group.

"Those women there," he said pointing.

Hoping to win Peter over, Kerrick expanded his chest. "Oh, those women are not a problem. I assure you the only color they are interested in is green. You're in my country now, my friend. Let me help you, like you will help me in America."

And like an African native leading other natives to the ship, which would take them to America, and eventually slavery, he beckoned the beauties in his direction with a wave of his hand. They floated to the table like moths to a flame.

When they stood above the men, their skin smelling like must and cheap perfume, Kerrick laid it on thick for show. "Why must you three do me and my friend the way you have all night? Can you be that cruel?"

The main one, also the thickest of the crew grinned. "And tell me, what exactly did we do?" She licked her lips and considered both men.

"You have single handedly taken us away from our business meeting. All we have been able to do was have lustful thoughts of you."

All of them giggled. "We're so sorry about that. Would you like us to stop?" the spokeswoman for the group responded.

"Never," Peter interjected.

Kerrick laughed and continued his play before his new white friend ruined it all. He was also using the opportunity to show he could talk slick and close the deal, despite not being in sales. "I'll tell you this, what do you say all of us grab some drinks and see where the night will lead us?"

The spokeswoman said, "That sounds like a plan to me."

The blue sky caught Kerrick as he walked through the door of his home. He hadn't done anything so disrespectful since he asked for Thandi's hand in marriage. Although a monster, he didn't play when it came to Thandi's love. He was consumed with guilt and would spend all night trying to convince her that this type of behavior would never happen again.

Besides, Kerrick wasn't interested in the other women. But Peter was and after entertaining the ladies at the club, he convinced Kerrick to stay with him until the sex act was done. Peter knew he couldn't handle all of the women by himself, but he refused to dismiss them either. So they rented a cheap motel, which stank of piss and old cum and got down to business. Surprisingly enough Peter was able to handle two women and Kerrick satisfied the third. He closed his eyes and envisioned his wife as he dipped in and out of her pussy but it didn't work. He felt awful and could not reach an orgasm. So he chose to fake it.

She was sexual and sensual but smelled of bad pussy and she had a habit of sucking his face, leaving scent trails of dried spit along the way, which resembled the odor of vinegar. Peter and Kerrick even had sex with one of the ladies at the same time and it was the closest he ever wanted to get with another man. It reminded him of darker days. The only thing he was thinking about was getting back to his dear wife.

The moment Kerrick opened the door leading to his house he knew something was off. The tiny hairs over his body stood on end and he was certain that Thandi was sitting in the living room waiting to take his head off.

He took a deep breath, pushed the door open further and prepared himself for his fate. But instead of seeing Thandi, he was met with silence. Death silence.

Hoping that she was asleep, so that he could creep into bed as if he'd been there the entire night, he continued down the hall leading toward their room.

When he happened upon the closed bedroom door, he pushed it open. What he saw next brought him to his knees. He was lightheaded and his heart pounded as he looked at the horrible scene before him.

Spread along the wall, above his bed, were the following words written in blood:

BABY KILLER, WE WAITED ALL NIGHT FOR YOU. SO WE TOOK YOUR WIFE INSTEAD. BUT WE WILL BE BACK.

Slowly his eyes rolled down to the blood soaked bed. He swallowed the lump in his throat and crawled toward the sheets. He snatched it off and it slid down slowly like it was doused in oil.

There, in the middle of the mattress was his wife's corpse. The murder was gruesome. Her throat was slit, her breasts were removed and placed over her eyes and her intestines hung out of her vagina.

Even in the condition she was in, Kerrick tried to pick himself up to hold her but he couldn't move. Instead he cried harder than a woman who had lost a child. He couldn't fathom living without his wife yet now he was forced to do so.

The rage. It had stolen any chance of him being human.

Which one of his victims was responsible? There was something sticking out of Thandi's mouth, between her teeth. He pulled himself up onto the bed and removed a red ribbon. His eyes widened and he touched his arm. It was the first time he realized he lost the ribbon that he placed on earlier yesterday.

It must have fallen off of his arm at Afua's house. Her husband was responsible and he had no doubt he would be back. After all, Kerrick had stolen his wife's life and his only child. He was sure Afua's husband would risk it all to seek revenge.

Kerrick eased onto the bed and lifted his wife's head. Blood soaked his clothing but he didn't care. He was already a monster but now he would be far more evil. He was certain that he would never love another woman like Thandi.

"Thandi, please forgive me," he cried. "I'm so sorry my secrets have caused you your life. And I will never love another like you. I just hope that you forgive me."

Afua was right, he would never touch his wife's lovely face again. Her beauty was stolen and ripped to shreds.

With a broken heart and mind, he knew he had to disappear to one place far away from his enemies.

America.

Kerrick walked down Reisterstown Road in Baltimore City on the way to the bus stop. He had been in America for three months and decided it was time to reach out to Peter Cramer, the man he shared drinks with at the club and a bed with in the motel with three beautiful whores.

When the bus arrived he paid his fare, stepped on and walked toward the back. Sitting next to the window he watched the landmarks and the structures exclusive to Baltimore appear and disappear as they drove by.

America had been unkind to Kerrick in the months he'd been there. He was ridiculed for his skin from the people who resembled him most. His accent was not as deep as the people in his country, because he had been working to sound more American all of his life, but it was still different. To make matters worse since his wife was murdered he couldn't focus in college and his grades suffered drastically. Things were so bad they were threatening to revoke his Visa.

It didn't take Kerrick long to learn that losing his wife had crippled him. He missed their long talks. He missed the way she smiled whenever he came home. He missed his life with her. But that life was over and he had to find a way to move on.

When he made it to the block where Cramer Construction and Associates stood, he rung the bell and got off of the bus. When he walked up on the building he was mesmerized. At the end of the block sat a gray building with gold accents, which stood as tall as the clouds. The words Cramer Construction glistened on the building's surface as the sun bounced off of the words.

Hopeful he pulled the large glass door open and walked up to the receptionist sitting behind a cream marble counter. Before approaching he glanced down at himself to be sure he was presentable. He was wearing blue slacks that rose dangerously close to his ankles and a white shirt that was riddled in wrinkles. Without his baby smuggling job he was broke and barely had enough money to buy anything to eat, let alone a new suit. Had it not been for the Thrift Store a block down from the room he rented he wouldn't have anything decent.

Kerrick grabbed the pen on the counter and his hand shook as he signed his name on the SIGN IN SHEET on the receptionists' desk. When he was done he dropped the pen and it rolled into her lap accidently. He was all thumbs. "I'm sorry," he said in a low voice, "I'm here to see Peter Cramer."

The receptionist's pale skin wrinkled on her forehead and her upper lip tightened, causing vertical dips. She picked up the pen and slammed it on the desk. "And you are?"

"Kerrick Khumalo."

"Is he expecting you?"

"Yes," he lied.

The woman scrutinized his crinkled attire and said, "One moment please." She grabbed the phone, dialed a few numbers and spoke to someone on the other end. She mastered the art of concealment because she spoke so low Kerrick couldn't make out a word she said. When she was done she slammed the phone down and said, "he doesn't know you." She proceeded to read the book on her desk.

Kerrick felt hollow inside. Although he met Peter once, he was sure that what they experienced in Zimbabwe would stay etched in his mind forever. Unless he slept with that many women in Africa with the help of a male native.

"I hate to bother you," he smiled. "But can you tell him I'm the engineer that introduced him to three friends one night in Mutare? South Africa? I'm sure he'll remember me then."

"He said he doesn't know you. Now unless there's anything else, I'm busy."

He observed the book and grew angry. "I understand," Kerrick said forcefully. "But it would be a shame for me to really be a friend only for you to be treating me so disrespectfully. I would hate to have to tell Cramer about your behavior once we reconnected. You could lose your job and I don't want that."

The receptionist rolled her eyes. She didn't think Peter would really fire her but not having a job was not a chance she was willing to take. Besides, how would she buy the pint sized vodka bottles she kept under her desk if she was unemployed?

More annoyed, she picked up the phone and whispered something into the handset. When she was done she slammed the phone down, scrutinized Kerrick and said, "He'll be down in a moment. Wait over there." She pointed to a burgundy leather sofa against the gray marble wall.

Kerrick ambled over to the couch and waited. An hour later the elevator dinged and Peter strutted out. He was dressed in a crisp brown designer suit, complete with the matching jacket. He had a jutting chin and when he spotted Kerrick he gave him a nod before placing a fake grin on his face.

Kerrick stood up to greet him.

Peter strolled up to Kerrick, extended his hand and said, "Hello, there." Kerrick shook his hand. "I see you found me, Kerrick."

Kerrick noticed how Peter wiped his hand after the shake and he tried not to get offended. He didn't recall Peter wiping his dick after they had sex with one of the women at the same time, or his balls when theirs touched.

Peter placed his hand on his chin as if he was pondering something.

"Yes, I have. I'm sorry if this is a bad time."

"That depends. What do you want?"

Kerrick caught his snappiness and was offended. But he made up his mind not to let his behavior destroy his opportunity. He was there for a job and he needed to remain professional. "I'm in town," Kerrick announced as if Peter wasn't aware.

"Good for you," he replied dryly and as equally uninterested.

"Well…I was hoping that you could use me in your engineering department. You know, like we talked about."

Peter stepped back and crossed his arms over his chest. "You finished college already?" he looked behind him to see who was watching him keep time with the strange African in the lobby.

"No, it's a long story," Kerrick laughed to ease the mood. "And I really don't need a degree because I know so much about the field already. Just give me a chance."

"Well to work for me you'll need a degree."

“Okay, I’ll get one.” Kerrick cleared his throat and his eyes roamed toward the angry receptionist who was staring over at them. “But you also said you could use interns.”

“Even if I could it wouldn’t be paid.”

“But I’m in a bind now. I’m living in a two-bedroom apartment with this woman who—,”

“We reached our quota, Kerrick,” he said cutting him off. “I really am sorry.”

Kerrick leaned in, not certain what he meant. “What does that mean?”

“It means that we’ve reached our minority quota for the year.”

“Minority quota?”

“Negro quota,” Peter yelled tiring of his guest. “Okay?” he paused. “Now we’ve hired enough negro’s for the year and aren’t interested in hiring anymore. Now I’m sure Nancy has your information. If something changes I will contact you but please do not come back here again.” He glanced him up and down. “You’re embarrassing.” Peter stuffed his hands in his pockets and stormed off.

Kerrick watched him until he walked on the elevator and disappeared from sight. He waited three months to visit him, until he was able to afford a suit and it was all for nothing. The disappointment weighed on him like an ant caught under a brick. The possibility of having that job was all he had to look forward to and now it was gone.

Angry at the world, he strolled toward the receptionist’s desk and looked down at her. She was certain that he was about to give her his personal information like Peter said in the conversation, and since she could tell by Peter's attitude that he didn't want to be bothered, her intention was to be extremely rude.

Kerrick placed his hands on the counter. His fist clutched and he glared down at her. "Back home I would take women like you and gut out your insides, while watching the blood roll from your body." He paused to allow his words to sink in. "If I ever see you alone on the street you will feel what I think about you in this moment. And it would be the most painful thing you ever experienced in your life. I guarantee it."

The receptionist looked into his eyes and her body shivered. She clamped her meaty thighs together to prevent from pissing on herself.

When he took her heart, and was sure his black face would haunt her dreams forever, he stuffed his hands in his pockets and walked away.

Kerrick knew after that utterance that he could never come back. He would have to think of another plan to be successful in America. What line of work could a man discover that would make him rich and powerful? He didn't have an answer but he was sure he would find it.

CHAPTER TWO
KERRICK
1966

AMERICA - BALTIMORE, MD

"He's sudden if a thing comes in his head."
-William Shakespeare

The heat was on blast making it hard to breathe in the small bedroom. Kerrick, who changed his name to Damien Trevor to prevent the immigration authorities from finding him because of an expired VISA, and to fit in with Americans with a more traditional name, was on a fragile twin size bed eating a seventy-year-old woman's pussy. Emma smelled of dried urine because she hadn't taken a bath in two days and she moaned so loudly he was certain his neighbors could hear her.

Kerrick did all he could to encourage her to bathe before she forced him into sexual predicaments, in lieu of rent, but nothing worked. He was starting to believe that she enjoyed having him do disgusting things in order to control him. And to see how badly he wanted to stay.

Her soft wrinkled legs were spread so far her bones cracked. "Lick it harder, Damien," she yelled. Her yellow hand slapped him in the face. "Get it good."

Kerrick slurped up her juices as he continued to earn his keep.

"That's right, bush nigger. Lap that pussy up. Lap it all up. And pull my sweet lips back and suck that button too."

Kerrick pushed the lips of her vagina back and her clit popped up like a tiny seed. White doughy substance surrounded her clitoris and he lowered his head and licked that too. His mouth tasted as if he'd eaten a raw onion and he wondered when it would be over so he could wash her taste from his mouth.

Emma grinned down at him because there was nothing the African wouldn't do to stay in her home. He was her handsome slave and she had all intentions on keeping it that way.

On the verge of an orgasm, she ordered him to lie on his back. Then she pushed her pussy into his face until he could not breathe. She rubbed her pussy against his lips until a powerful orgasm squeezed out and placed a smile on her face.

When she was done, he rushed into the bathroom, vomited and took a shower. He took one earlier in the day but when she stopped him at the living room door, right before he was scheduled for work, he knew he wouldn't be comfortable unless he took another. When he was done with the shower he brushed his teeth and mouth so hard his tongue bled.

What had his life become?

Clean, he slid into his clothes, grabbed his wallet off the dresser and left out of his room. Emma was sitting on the sofa pointing a huge remote control at the television. She stopped when she rested on the soap opera *Guiding Light.* A velvet robe was draped over her body and her hand clutched a beer.

"Where are you going?" she asked never removing her eyes off of the television. She widened her legs so that he could get another look at her vagina if he so desired.

Disgusted, Kerrick moved toward the door. "It doesn't matter, Emma. I've taken care of you already. I'm done."

She rolled her head in his direction. "Don't get sassy with me, Bush Nigger. The only reason you're in my apartment is because I have allowed you to stay. Now I asked you a question, where are you going?"

Frustrated he let out a loud sigh. Before answering he glanced over at a picture on the wall of Emma when she was younger. Before age and years of cigarette smoking attacked her face, she was a beautiful woman. And not as lonely.

Forty years ago she was married to Todd Jenkins, a banker who made quite a living for himself by investing in the Dot Com industry. But living in racist Mississippi made life difficult for the wealthy African American couple so they knew they had to move.

After some thought Todd and Emma relocated to the east coast, hoping that Baltimore City would welcome them. For a while they were both pleased and life was good. Todd continued to invest in stocks and bonds and Emma found refuge in catering benefits for special events.

But her husband had another fetish, big fat women with dark skin and thick asses. During the day he roamed around the city with his beautiful fare skinned wife but at night there wasn't a brothel in DC, Maryland or Virginia that didn't welcome him home. Emma knew about her husband's infidelities but she turned a blind eye. Besides, she wasn't about to give up her home to some whore and be turned on the streets. His money belonged to her.

Instead she took care of her man, even when he caught HIV and died a violent death. It was Emma who nursed his wounds, cleaned his bedpans and made sure he didn't want for anything. Despite knowing that his lifestyle could have placed her at risk of catching the virus too.

When he died she gave up her passion for catering and picked up drinking and smoking instead. Her heart hardened and she made it known that love was the last thing she wanted. At least that's what she told herself.

Although she was still wealthy, one would never know. She stayed in one of the apartments she owned and barely left the place. Instead she would pick the man of her choosing, make him do unspeakable acts of sex until she put him out or they grew tired and left.

But Kerrick, or Damien as she knew him, lasted longer than any of her other tenants, and she was starting to develop feelings for him. Something was driving the man and giving him the strength to deal with her. He was unstoppable and focused on his goal.

"I'm going to work, Emma," Kerrick said calmly. "I'll see you later."

She placed her beer down and grabbed a cigarette. "Yeah, well, stop by my room before you go to sleep." She grinned. "I'm feeling womanly right now and may need you to take care of me again."

She ran her hand up her thigh and he walked out without responding.

Kerrick washed dishes in the kitchen of Mama's Kitchen. He was over an hour late thanks to Emma and was concerned that he would lose his job. He landed the gig after being turned down at five other restaurants due to people feeling uncomfortable with employees with cultural differences. He not only wanted this job but he needed it. The plan was to save up enough money to rent his own apartment but he was a long way off.

He was on his last pan when Victoria Fole walked up behind him. She was a tall blond haired white woman with large brown eyes and a breathtaking smile. She was also Kerrick's manager. "Damien, can I talk to you for a minute?" she asked in a soft angelic voice. "It won't take long."

He turned around and grabbed the hand towel hanging on the edge of the sink. "Sure. Let me put this pan up and I'll be right in your office."

"Okay."

When she left he sighed and looked out into the dining area through the window above the sink. The diner was always packed and he hoped that fact would be a reason for Victoria, and the people at the corporate office, to allow him to keep his job.

When he was done he dried his hands on the towel and walked past the water cooler sitting on the side of the wall and knocked on Victoria's door.

"Come in, Damien," she said softly.

Kerrick entered, smiled at her and took a seat in front of her desk as he waited for the verdict. She didn't have any pictures of family members on her desk and he wondered why.

Victoria shuffled some papers around and nothing seemed in order. Her fingers trembled as she asked, "Damien, were you late today?" her eyes remained on the mess, not Kerrick.

He wanted to lie but was certain that she pulled the video footage by now. "Yes, and I'm very sorry."

She exhaled and looked up at him. "But why? They told you what would happen if you were late again. I thought you liked working here."

"I do."

"Then why must you continuously come late?"

Kerrick could have told her a million lies, each one of them having zero meaning. But he decided to go another route. "Have I ever told you how beautiful you are?" A sly smile rested on his face.

"Damien, please don't..."

"I'm serious, Victoria," he responded walking in front of her chair. He sat on the desk and looked down at her as if he were the boss. In one instant she had become his subordinate. "Whenever I see you I can never take my eyes off of you." They fooled around once before and she tried to resist it from happening again.

"You're just saying that."

"In my country men don't say what they don't believe," he responded.

"Oh, Damien," she said as she breathed hard.

"It's true. When I become a wealthy man I'm going to take care of you, Victoria. I told you before and I'm telling you again." He raised his arms by his sides and allowed them to fall. "I know you look at me and see a dishwasher. But if you look a little deeper you'll see a king. And I will be your husband. I will make your dreams come true."

Victoria's heart pounded and she wanted nothing more than to believe him. She was both a fool and a hopeless romantic. "Please stop, Damien." Her breaths were deep and rapid. "I'm going to lose my job."

"And you know I don't want that. I just want to make you feel good for your troubles." He dropped to his knees and placed his rough hands on her bare thighs. He pushed her dress toward her waist and revealed her cotton white panties. He moved them to the side, lowered his head snaked his tongue around her clit. It hardened with each stroke. When she was nice and wet he stiffened his tongue and entered her pussy hole back and forth as if he were making love to her. She tasted way better than the old bag. He learned one thing about being in the US. And it was that American women loved their kitties licked.

Victoria, unable to resist, gripped his head and maneuvered her hips. She eyed the door every so often and prayed nobody would enter. How could she explain herself.

Kerrick could care less who entered. He didn't stop until she was clawing at his back and she was cumming inside of his mouth.

When he was done he raised is head and looked into her eyes. "I am going to take care of you, Victoria. I just ask that you look out for me now."

"But what do you want me to do?" she asked, her chest rising and falling like an ocean wave. "How can I explain why you still have a job when you continuously come in late?"

Kerrick walked to his seat and sat down. He clasped his hand on top of the desk and said, "Pick up the phone, Victoria. And make the call." He handed it to her. "You know what you have to say."

Victoria continued to work to slow down her breaths. When she was calmer she called the number to reach her boss. When the receptionist answered she said, "Jack Jacobs please." She eyed Kerrick as she waited. "Hello, Jack." She moved uncomfortably in her seat. "This is Victoria from the Baltimore diner."

"What can I do for you, Victoria?"

"I'm calling about my employee, Damien Trevor. I wanted to let you know that there has been a terrible mistake. He was at work the entire time."

Papers shuffled in the background. "But the morning manager said he hadn't come. Are you sure?"

"I'm certain, Mr. Jacobs. I'm not sure why Anna didn't see him. But I have his timesheet here if you need to see it."

He sighed. "No, I don't. Just have Anna call me in the morning. I'll find out what's going on then."

When she disconnected she pinched the skin on her throat until it reddened in several areas. It was a nervous habit of hers. This was not good. She could feel it.

When her boss called to speak to Anna she was going to dispute his absence vehemently. "I'm going to get fired, Damien," she said softly, on the verge of tears.

"No you won't, Victoria. Just unplug the machine like you did the last time and make everybody sign in and out for breaks. That way we can tell them that the time clock was unplugged by mistake." He knew she was naive and he needed to use this character flaw to his advantage. She had been that way all of her life.

Victoria was born to an Irish father and an Italian mother. They drank hard and fought harder. Gianna, Victoria's mother, and her father Pearce, met at a Pizzeria in Brooklyn New York. Since both of them were employees and worked the night shift they spent a lot of time together. It was inevitable that they met and fell in love.

The only problem was that Gianna had a mean streak like no other. Out of jealousy she once accused Pearce of fucking his own mother and spread the rumor around the Pizzeria and their neighborhood. Pearce never discovered where the rumor originated but it made him stray from his mother to prove everyone wrong. He didn't want them whispering and drawing conclusions.

A short time after that, Gianna and Pearce rented a tiny one-bedroom apartment where they discovered their love of Scotch. They were drunk so much that Gianna didn't know she was pregnant until she was in labor with Victoria. Both of her parents died five years ago after driving drunk. It was a classic end to their marriage.

Victoria was born with alcohol in her system and as a result she often forgot things and was very impressionable. The only reason she was made manager of Mama's Kitchen was because she would do whatever the owner wanted and he wouldn't be forced to sit through her opinion or what she thought about a matter.

Now that Kerrick had her under his spell he could move her like a puppet and she would do anything he wanted. He started to believe that, that was the kind of woman he needed in his life. One with no backbone.

There was another reason Kerrick wanted to keep Victoria around. He was starting to believe that with a white woman on his arm society would look at him in a positive light. He would be perceived as a man with wealth and may even be respected. He worked overtime to fit into the American image of what he should be. His accent was vanishing and he had even begun to bleach his skin.

"I'll unplug the time clock but are you sure they won't fire me?" she relented.

"You have to trust me, Victoria," he coached. "I wouldn't steer you wrong. Ever. From here on out I will be your master and you will be my woman." Kerrick stood up and walked toward the door. Before he left the office he turned around and said, "It's okay for you to fall in love with me. I will never hurt you."

The fear she felt about losing her job was replaced with idolization. He said the right thing at the right time and Victoria felt safe. She lived to be dominated.

With her help he was able to keep his job at the moment but he knew that wouldn't last because of the freak he lived with. He needed to find a way to earn enough money to move and make his American dream come true. Washing dishes wasn't going to cut it.

When he left he walked toward the large sink he worked at. More dishes were piled high and waited on him to clean them. He was an educated man forced to do the work fitting of a high school drop out. He was blown.

Kerrick picked up a pan and began to scrub it. When he stared out ahead of him through the window he saw five teenagers draped in expensive clothing. One of them sat on the end and a stack of one hundred dollar bills was stuffed in the palm of his hands.

In Kerrick's eyes he looked like he was a part of the American dream.

"What do you do for a living?" he said to himself. "I'm going to find out."

CHAPTER THREE
KERRICK

"No beast so fierce but knows some touch of pity."
-William Shakespeare

Kerrick was lying face up on his bed as he waited on Victoria to walk out of the bathroom. His gray sweat-pants couldn't hide his growing hard on. But today was more about business than it was sex. Besides, there was not a woman alive who could satisfy him as well as Thandi could.

Still, he brought Victoria to his apartment because three days ago he almost lost his job and thanks to her he was still gainfully employed. He started envisioning his life with her on his arm and suddenly things were looking good.

Yes. Victoria would be his trophy wife.

When she walked out of the bathroom, Kerrick's thick burgundy towel was wrapped around her waist. She wasn't wearing a bra. She looked at him. She seemed hesitant. Sensing her apprehension Kerrick got up and walked her over to the bed. Once there he sat on the tiny mattress and it squeaked. She stood in front of him and waited for his next command.

"Take it off."

She released the towel and watched it flop to the floor. He ran his hand over her thigh. Amazed at the contrast of her white skin against his dark hand.

Victoria moaned. Although he fingered her a few times at the job and ate her pussy once or twice, this would be the first time they would be making love.

Kerrick slid his hand from her navel to her warm vagina. He stroked her bulging clit and it moistened quickly. He was about to kiss her kitty until the bedroom door flew open.

When Kerrick looked at the intruder he was staring into the red-hot face of Emma. His eyes traced her crinkled lips and trailed down to the butcher knife that dangled in her hand. "What is this white bitch doing in my house?" She squalled.

Kerrick hopped up and said, "Put your clothes on, Victoria."

She quickly obeyed as she bumbled around the room looking for her left and right shoe.

"I said what is she doing in my house?" Emma questioned once more.

Sensing that danger was imminent, Kerrick grabbed his white shirt off the floor. He pulled it down over his head and quickly placed his arms through the armholes so that he could see Emma in case she made a move. "She's my friend. I am allowed to have company. I pay rent right?"

Emma burst into laughter and regarded him closely. "Pay rent? Does your lily white girlfriend know what you do to earn your keep around here?" she wielded the knife back and forth. She was so jealous it was foolish.

"You need to calm down," he warned.

"I get it, she's here to help you out huh?" Emma raised the edge of the robe, revealing her bushy gray pussy hairs. "Well get over here, Lily. I'm waiting."

Kerrick grabbed Victoria's hand and his silver queen plant and rushed toward the bedroom door. But the old woman was relentless and blocked their path.

"Move, Emma," he warned. "I'm leaving."

"If you leave you can never come back."

"I'm leaving for good."

The sly smile rinsed off her face. She didn't want him to leave…ever. She cared about him. "Where you gonna live rent free huh? Won't nobody take a bush nigger in off the street but me."

"Emma, I'm asking you to move. I won't tell you again."

"Not until you—

With a stiff arm Kerrick gripped her throat, pressing his thumb against her right carotid artery while his other fingers pushed against the left. He squeezed slowly and firmly. Before long the knife fell out of her hand and stabbed into the floor.

When her eyes closed he released her and watched her drop to the ground.

He looked down at her body and said, "Wherever I'm going isn't your problem no more. Now you know."

Kerrick stood over the sink in Mama's Kitchen, washing dishes as he thought about Thandi. He missed her so much that it was sickening. Two weeks ago he moved out of Emma's apartment and he was now living with Victoria.

Emma didn't die that night but she was hospitalized for three days. When it got back to Kerrick that she might press charges for assault, he visited her in the hospital. She was asleep when she felt someone massaging her throat. When Emma opened her eyes, Kerrick was standing over top of her like a ghost. He vowed to get it right the next time he choked her if he heard she was talking to police. Emma finally got to see what kind of man Kerrick was. A dangerous one. And it scared her enough to leave him the fuck alone.

Kerrick had no idea that Victoria had her own place. He assumed that someone as naive as she was would have someone taking care of her. She lived in a tiny one-bedroom apartment, big enough for the few clothes he owned and his plant. He knew it wouldn't be the end of his journey in America but it was a start.

Kerrick wasted no time taking over Victoria's life. The first thing he did was to convince her to let him handle all the bills. She agreed, with the first order of business being to hand over her paychecks each month. She didn't mind especially since Kerrick was dicking her down proper-like.

He was on his last pan when the same thugs he saw come into the restaurant some weeks back returned. The apparent leader was six foot four and hovered over the rest of the group. His black shirt acted as a backdrop to the large platinum medallion outlined in diamonds swinging from his neck. He took a seat and the other four sat in chairs surrounding him as if to protect him.

A few moments later the leader waved a waitress over to place his order. Kerrick couldn't take his eyes off him and he wondered what kind of power he possessed.

When the meals were served, Kerrick continued to spectate. The water was cold and more dishes were piling on the countertop around him but who cared. He wanted in on the business. He could see the man had money but the problem was finding a good way to introduce himself. So when the leader made a comment to a female at another table, and her boyfriend got upset, he saw his opportunity.

"You have another position for your eyes, or do you want me to redirect them for you?" the Boyfriend asked the Leader at the table with his mob.

The Leader smirked and said, "You seem real upset about a bitch who can't stop looking over here. Maybe you should check your girl."

"I wasn't looking over there," the loud mouthed but sexy woman responded. She pawed at her long flowing black weave, rolled her eyes and turned away from him.

"Even if she was looking at you, you ain't answer my question," the Boyfriend continued. "Do you need help readjusting your eyes?" It was obvious that he was ready to fight and the Leader was intimidated.

"Is there something I can help you with gentlemen?" Kerrick asked the Leader before looking at the Boyfriend.

The Boyfriend observed the African native, laughed and said, “Naw, I’m good.” He placed his arm around the woman’s shoulder and proceeded to enjoy the rest of his meal.

Kerrick assumed everything was over but the Leader’s eyes told him otherwise. He didn’t like how the Boyfriend had dismissed him in front of his squad. He felt he violated but was too afraid to do something about it. He was one of them fake ass thugs the world knew all too well.

“What about you, sir? Can I help you with anything?”

The Leader looked up at Kerrick and said, “Naw, you not up for it. Now get the fuck out my face.” He turned his attention to his crew but Kerrick wouldn’t budge. He stood like a historic New York City building. He stood tried, true and strong. “What do you want, African?” the Leader yelled looking up at him. “I said get the fuck up out my face.”

“You said I’m not up for it. I want to prove to you I am. What would you like me to do?

The Leader finally considered Kerrick. His uniform gave off the misconception of dishwasher but his stance whispered…killer.

The Leader readjusted in his seat and said, “Okay, first what do you want from me?”

“A chance to make money. To live the American dream like you. That’s all I ask.”

The Leader nodded. “Okay, okay. I hear you.” He looked over at the Boyfriend who hadn’t given him a second look since him and his girlfriend gave him their backs. "The dude over there disrespected me. I want that handled." He was certain that the dishwasher would run after hearing what he desired.

"Any particular method?" Kerrick questioned.

"Just make it violent."

Kerrick repositioned himself and walked toward the back of the restaurant. "I knew the nigga was a punk," the Leader chided. "Just what I thought.

But when Kerrick returned with a butcher knife large enough to slice a human head in half, he was prepared to eat his words.

Kerrick gently tapped the Boyfriend on the back and when he turned around, he swiped over his face with the blade, slicing into the outer corners of his eye while severing his nose completely off.

Blood splattered on Kerrick's apron and his girlfriend's new hairdo. She ran out of Mama's Kitchen leaving him alone. It was every bitch for herself. A few other patrons dashed toward the exit, unsure of what the African native would do next. The Leader stood up from the table, frozen, until his men rushed him toward the exit before the police came.

In the end no one remained in the dining room except Kerrick and his screaming victim.

But before long there would be police and a sentence of five years to keep Kerrick company.

CHAPTER FOUR
KERRICK
1971

"So wise so young, they say, do never live long."
-William Shakespeare

When the gates opened the clinking noise was music to twenty-three year old Kerrick's ears. He looked up at the sapphire sky and squinted. He couldn't believe he was free. After five years in prison he was going home. It had been a long road. And a violent one too. Not only did he have to fight to gain his respect, he was worried that the prison authorities would learn that he wasn't Damien Trevor, but Kerrick Khumalo, an immigrant from Zimbabwe with an expired VISA.

He didn't mind the slaughterhouse battles in prison, or the altercations that gained him a gash across the neck and down his left thigh. The only thing he feared was being shipped back to Africa without making his mark in America. If he failed everything would be in vain, including the mauling of his wife Thandi. He had to become a success. He had to become king.

When he swaggered out of the gate he saw a silver Volkswagen van with the engine running. The driver's door opened and a beautiful Latino woman with long brown hair stepped in front of the vehicle. She took a moment to observe Kerrick and then as if on queue, tears streamed down her face. She couldn't believe he was free. She covered her mouth with her trembling hands and wept into them.

Kerrick stood solid, never showing his emotion. He learned to use coldness inside of the pen and he would keep that trait throughout life, no matter whom he was dealing with.

When he moved closer to the woman, the sound of his boots stepping on the dirt crackled until he stopped and was standing in front of her.

He was calm but the beauty couldn't take it anymore. She snatched him toward her and embraced him passionately. But it was as if she was hugging a teddy bear that could not hold her back. Her plush breasts pressed against his chiseled chest. Her body trembled as she held the man she dreamed of for the past two years. When she gained her composure she released him and looked into his eyes, "Damien, I can't believe it's you."

"Francesca." His eyes wheeled up and down her body. "You're as beautiful as I remembered."

It had been two years since he'd seen Francesca in person. Mainly because she belonged to another man and could not visit. He and Francesca met in a peculiar way.

She had been visiting an inmate, Money Mouse, a drug dealer from Michigan, while Kerrick was with Victoria. The entire visit Francesca couldn't hear what her boyfriend was saying because she was too busy lusting after Kerrick.

It wasn't because he did anything spectacular or that he was so good looking. She found him irresistible because he carried himself like a Prince. Like everything happening around him didn't faze him in the least. In prison he was God or God-like. And she was a sucker for men with power.

Every week for the next year Francesca visited Money Mouse, a man she met through a Pen Pal organization. But after some time it had become obvious to everyone, that she had eyes for Kerrick.

Unable to win a battle against Kerrick, and needing to save himself the embarrassment, Money Mouse told Francesca never to visit him again. Part of him wanted to step to the bold African but while Kerrick was in jail he associated with natives from his homeland, who were all killers and were ready to fight for the love of Africa.

Before long Francesca was writing Kerrick and he wrote back. In each note she pledged her allegiance once he was set free. She claimed there wasn't a thing he could ask that wouldn't be done. She even gave him a contract for her soul and signed it in her blood. And after all the years, she never gave her body to another man. So when it came to sex she was way overdue.

After the greetings were over Francesca drove away from the prison while Kerrick observed everything around him. He hadn't been in the states long but he was now a changed man. He now viewed Americans as being beneath him and intellectually he believed that if he tried hard enough he could rule the world. He came from Africa and as a result his blood was uncontaminated to hear him tell it. And the African Americans in the United States were nothing more than glorified cotton pickers.

After the long drive to Francesca's home, in a suburb of Maryland, Kerrick took a bath and thought about his next steps. When he was done he walked into the bedroom and she dried him off before rubbing lotion over his body. Her touch, although sensual could not break him from his thoughts. He was a man on a mission.

"Your body is perfect," she admitted.

He grinned and said, "Thank you."

Although focused on his plans he gave his aspirations a break when Francesca raised his foot and ran her warm, wet tongue around each of his toes. His dick stiffened and the fire he suppressed in prison, because it could not be fulfilled, returned powerfully.

He was a man and she was a woman. It was time to attack.

Like a lioness preparing to kill her prey, she crawled over top of him. She lowered herself until her warm box smothered his throbbing manhood. Kerrick bucked into her hard and at first it appeared he was angry because he was so rough. But when the fire in his eyes burned bright it was obvious that he was enjoying being inside of a woman. Beating his dick year after year could go but so far.

Unwilling to cum after only two minutes, Kerrick flipped her over and pounded her from behind. Her creamy skin against his chocolate dick looked picturesque. He pressed his hands on her lower back so that her belly touched the bed and her ass rose in the air. Once he had explored every inch of her, only then did he explode.

Satisfied with the experience, he slipped out of her and lie faced up on the bed. The black lacquer ceiling fan spinning over his head hypnotized him for a moment. Suddenly he was reunited with his thoughts again and he felt at home. How would he go about becoming a rich man? Was the question.

Feeling the disconnection, Francesca placed her head on his chest and played with a strand of his coarse hair. "Damien, I've been thinking. I mean, I know you can live anywhere you want. But I was hoping that you would stay here with me."

"You got any money?" he asked disregarding her statement.

"Sure…uh…how much do you need?"

"All you got."

Fran eased out of bed and switched toward the dresser. Her hair cascaded down the middle of her back and she resembled a model. She was hoping that Kerrick would view her curvy body and be inclined to stay for the rest of his life. Instead he paid her no attention. "Here you go," she said extending three hundred dollars. "It's all I have on me right now."

He snatched the money, hopped out of bed and got dressed. When he walked out of the room and strutted to the front door like he had just been paid for his services, she felt humiliated. She was right behind him and before he left out he asked, "Can I use your van?" He picked a few pieces of lint off of the shirt he was wearing.

Her mouth opened and at first nothing came out. She was surprised at how he was treating her. "But how will I get to work?"

"What about your best friend?" he yawned. "When you wrote me you said she lived down the street. Call her."

She moved uneasily in front of him. Who was he? He acted so differently than the man who wrote her just to trap her mind. "Damien, I don't know if I can—"

He immediately grew angry and his brows lowered. "You said you would be willing to do anything for me."

"And I am."

"Well do this one thing and I will take care of you for the rest of your life. But if you deny me I want you to remember this moment. Always."

Fran took a few moments to think about her decision. She glanced around, avoiding eye contact with him. She spent so many days thinking about their lives together that she didn't want to be without him. So with hunched shoulders she walked toward her room and returned with the van keys. "Can you at least tell me where you are going?" She handed them to him.

"I have some things to care for. But I'll call you when I'm settled so I can bring your van back. A few days at the most."" He placed a knot of her loose hair behind her ear. "Thank you for being loyal." He winked and walked away. Leaving her with a dripping pussy and a broken heart.

After going to a pawnshop Kerrick pulled up at Victoria's tiny house in Baltimore city. It had been six months since he'd seen her at the prison, because she took on two jobs to raise enough money to buy him new clothes and a car once he was released.

Life had been hard since Kerrick was arrested. She didn't have the job at Mama's Kitchen anymore because they learned that she had been altering Kerrick's time-sheet. To make ends meet she took on a job as a waitress at another diner and at nights she bartended at a local club. But for Kerrick she would have done more.

When Kerrick made it to the house, he looked behind him for strangers and lifted the red mat. He removed the key opened the door and entered the house. Everything was clean and it smelled of lavender. Although the furniture was shabby, Victoria kept a clean home and her love for him was displayed everywhere. Pictures from their visits had been blown up and placed in nice frames on the wall and smaller versions sat on the living room table.

Exhausted he walked to the bedroom and sat on the edge of the bed. Everything was as neat in the room as it was in the living room and he felt at home.

When something caught his eye on the table at the side of the bed he picked it up. It was a pink envelope with the words *I Love You* written on the top. He opened it slowly and read Victoria's words:

Damien,

I have been waiting for this day for five years. To hold you again and to have you back in my life. I feel horrible that I'm not there to share your first moments of freedom. I'll be home soon.

PS. There are new clothes waiting for you in the closet. And I made a turkey sandwich for you. It's in the fridge.

Kerrick took a shower ate his sandwich and took a nap. After making love to Francesca and running a few errands he was spent. When he woke up, about two hours later he was staring into Victoria's eyes. He stood up and hugged her as she sobbed uncontrollably in his arms.

Unlike when he saw Francesca, he greeted her with a secure hug. He planted a kiss on her face and looked deeply into her eyes. "I need you to stop crying because I want to ask you something. But you must think clearly before saying yes."

"Of course, Damien." She wiped her tears with her fingertips.

"Your loyalty is amazing. And it kept me alive in prison. So I want you by my side for the next level of my life." He took her small head into his hands and gripped it while he stared deeper into her eyes. "Victoria, would you do me the honor of being my wife?"

Victoria's face reddened and her eyes expanded when she heard the big question. From the moment she first met him at Mama's Kitchen she loved him more than her own self-respect and life. "Of course," she said emphatically. "I want nothing more than to live for you."

Kerrick reached into his pants and pulled out a small black box that he'd gotten from the pawnshop. He got the money from Fran and although the ring was small he had plans to buy her a larger one when his plans for kingdom came through.

Taking her hand into his, he lowered on one knee and looked up at her. He slipped it on her finger and surprisingly it was the right fit.

When the ring was secure, he stood up and gazed into her eyes. "The diamond is small. But if you stick with me, I'll put a bigger one on it when I make our dreams come true."

"I don't care, Damien. All I want you to do is love me. More than you loved any other woman."

Kerrick frowned and he immediately thought about Thandi. What Victoria asked him was impossible. "I love you, Victoria. I really do. But I will never love you as much as you want me to. That place in my heart has already been taken." He paused. "Can you deal with that?"

Her body tensed upon hearing his words but she had no choice. Kerrick was the only man for her. "Yes."

"Good," he smiled pleased she was willing to take second place.

"So when do you want to do this?"

Not being a man of patience he fervently announced, "Tomorrow."

A few days later the sun lit up the old black Volkswagen Beetle Victoria bought Kerrick at an auction. She saved up just enough money to buy him a bucket but it was reliable and he cared about her for it.

As he drove down the street he contemplated over and over that he was a married man. He hoped he wasn't being disloyal to Thandi with his vows. He didn't even marry her with his real name. He knew the wedding at the courthouse was not what Victoria had in mind but he had a plan and wanted everything executed.

When he glanced up at the Greenmount Avenue street sign a dopehead had given him earlier when he asked where could he find Yori, he parked the car. Although he and Yori only met once, Kerrick did five years for him in prison and wanted to request an audience. In Kerrick's mind not only had he proven his loyalty when he slashed Marcus Camp's face, and severed his nose, he felt Yori also owed him a favor.

When Kerrick first made it to prison Yori would put money on his books in the hopes that if Kerrick beat the case he would come and work for him. Besides, a goon as vicious as Kerrick came once in a lifetime and he needed him on the cold streets of Baltimore. But his good Samaritan behavior ended when he was made aware how much time Kerrick received. Had it been a year Yori would've continued his charade, but courting a goon for five years seemed outlandish. So the money stopped.

Kerrick didn't mind much. He was appreciative that Yori did what he could for as long as he did. And it wasn't like he didn't have Victoria and Fran in his corner. His books stayed straight and his commissary account stayed full. But now that he was free he wanted the riches he felt he was due.

Kerrick approached a group of five men who were talking in a huddle in front of a red row home. They seemed unaware of the monster approaching them. Kerrick felt that was a bad move at best. Had he been a man with less than honorable intentions, the five of them would've been face down kissing concrete.

Kerrick observed the pack. Although he couldn't see their faces he knew which one was Yori. He studied him so much at Mama's Kitchen that he memorized his gait and how he carried himself. So he stepped to him.

"Yori," Kerrick said plainly with his hand stuffed in his jean pockets. "I'm home."

At first Yori spun around in an aggressive manner, prepared to deal with whoever thought they knew him enough to call his name and interrupt his conversation. But when he saw it was Kerrick his expression softened. There was a smidgen of uncertainty behind his glare, because he didn't know if Kerrick was angry that he was given five years on account of him. But he would try to fake it.

With a wide counterfeit smile on his face, Yori yelled, "I know that's not my nigga, Damien." He jogged down the few steps it took to greet Kerrick eye to eye. He pulled him into a masculine embrace and slapped him hard on the back. When he released him he asked, "When did you get home, brother?"

"A few days ago."

Yori stepped back and frowned. He placed his fingers on his chin as if he was pondering what Kerrick had just said. “Hold up, why you didn’t hit me up earlier? I would’ve brought you home right.” He looked at Kerrick’s clean but off brand gear.

“I had to see my ladies first,” Kerrick said calmly. “But I’m here now.”

“Did you hear this cat,” Yori announced loudly to the other men on the top of the step. “This cat said he had to see his bitches.” He slapped Kerrick on his shoulder. “Right on, my brother. Get pussy first.”

Kerrick nodded but was growing weary of Yori’s antics. He couldn’t believe that he was in charge of anything because he didn’t carry himself like a boss. Still, he was the one who could change his life and Kerrick had to humble himself or he would lose out on the American Dream.

“So what are you doing here?” Yori asked.

“I need a job. I’m a hard worker and I hope I’ve demonstrated my ability to follow orders already.”

“Did you demonstrate your ability to follow orders?” he repeated. “Fuck yeah you did.” He looked back at the men again. “Let my man be a lesson to the rest of you worthless niggas. He did five years off of the strength of an order I gave him and never batted an eye. That’s an assassin.” When he was done with his staging, he addressed Kerrick again. “Of course you’ve proven what you can do. And even though the streets are dry these days, I should be able to find work for you.”

Kerrick was pleased because up to that point he wasn’t sure if he would get played again like he did when he visited Peter Cramer when he first arrived in America.

A smile, which was uncommon for Kerrick, appeared on his face. “Thank you, man. You know I got you. So what do you need me as? Muscle?”

Yori leaned back and said, “Whoa. You have to practice before you can spar with the champs.” He turned around and yelled, “Aye, Mox. Bring me that pack.”

A fat kid, who was eating a taco, stuffed what was left into his mouth. He then observed his surroundings as if he wasn’t already slipping, and reached into a Doritos bag on the porch. He removed a plastic bag and handed it to Yori.

Yori took it from him. “This right here is HAIR-RON. You move this and you got a job for life, you dig?” He handed it to Kerrick.

Kerrick examined the large Ziploc that was stuffed with tinier heroin bags. “I’m confused. You want me to be a…”

“Instrumental part of our business,” Yori said finishing his sentence. “There ain’t no money being made without the foot soldiers. Empty that work and I’ll see what else I got for you. Deal?”

Kerrick didn’t have a choice. He was broke. He was unemployed. And he wanted in on the sensational lifestyle he’d seen on television as a child in Africa.

So he extended his hand and shook Yori’s. “Deal.”

CHAPTER FIVE
KERRICK

"I am not in the giving vein today."
-William Shakespeare

Kerrick was standing on the corner smoking a jack. For some reason when he approached Yori he never envisioned that he would be reduced to corner nigga status. In his country when a man demonstrated his ability to go the extra mile like he had at the restaurant, he would be rewarded in kind. That wasn't the case in America and it only added to one of the many reasons he despised the country he was trying to love.

Kerrick had been working for Yori for weeks. Whenever he was given a pack he moved it like it was nothing, making the other soldiers look incompetent in the process. But Kerrick was tired of the position. It wasn't challenging enough. And he decided to step to Yori about it later.

It was midnight when Yori finally stopped by to check on things. Kerrick let him talk to the other soldiers first and collect the money they owed before he spoke to him. When Yori finally walked over to Kerrick he readied himself for the conversation.

"Here's the money," Kerrick said handing Yori his cut. "I earned more this week than last."

Yori counted the money by licking his index finger and flipping bill after bill. "I see…I see. You have definitely proven yourself yet again."

"I'm glad you feel that way. Because I wanted to talk to you about getting another position."

"Damn, blood," Yori yelled. "Why you keep coming at me about the same shit? I said I'ma change your position when the time is right. If I haven't done it yet it means it ain't the right time."

Kerrick's left arm tightened and he was about to hold Yori's neck in his hand to see how soft it was. But when a large Mercedes Benz pulled up and parked, his attention was diverted. For the moment anyway.

Kerrick watched as a man with a huge build eased out of the backseat. His driver followed him.

Yori's entire disposition changed when the man's boot stepped on the block. He seemed less confrontational. Almost cowardly.

He was the boss not Yori. Kerrick was now certain.

"How are things going?" the Boss asked Yori.

"Things are fine, Abraham." He handed him the money he collected from the soldiers. "Everything is in order and the turn around has been quick."

Abraham thumbed through the stack. "I see profits are up too."

Kerrick seemed invisible as they continued to talk. He was infuriated. When Kerrick realized the man who he had done five years for was not the boss, he felt like strangling him on sight. Yori was nothing more than a glorified minion. Had he known this he would've requested to speak to Abraham weeks ago. But he also knew now was not the time. There were levels.

Abraham chewed Yori out about Chill, one of their soldiers who got robbed and killed last week. Riley was supposed to be with him but Yori let him off to go over his girl's house. Because of that the jacker got away with a nice stack of cash and the young dealer's work and jewelry. Abraham warned him if it happened again, Yori would be through in Baltimore if not dead.

When Abraham left Yori was upset. Kerrick walked closer to him and said, "Is he in charge of—"

Kerrick's sentence was cut short when Yori turned around and slapped him so hard Kerrick stumbled backwards. The pain rippled through his cheek and the embarrassment was more than he ever had to endure in a lifetime. But instead of going off, like Yori thought, Kerrick smiled. This intimidated Yori even more.

"Get back to…to…to work, Damien," he stuttered worried the man would kill him when he saw the fire in his eyes. "Before you be…be looking for work in DC."

Kerrick walked away from Yori without another word.

Francesca pleaded with Kerrick to be gentle on her body but her request fell on deaf ears. Infuriated with how Yori treated him he took it out on her sexually. He would've never treated his wife, who Francesca found out about last week, so viciously.

In her mind if she made herself available, he would realize he made a mistake by choosing Victoria, and marry her instead.

Kerrick drove into her pale buttocks forcefully and blood saturated the sheets beneath them as she begged for mercy. But he was unresponsive.

Brief memories of Yori's hand touching his face flashed in his mind on repeat and he went animalistic. Sweat poured down his face in puddles as he teetered the line between consensual sex and rape.

When he bust his nut inside of her, he pulled out his bloody penis and wiped it on her back. She defecated on the bed automatically because he tore her anus.

"Oh my god," she said embarrassed at her actions.

Without asking if she was okay, he got up, went to the bathroom and washed up. When he was done he slipped into his jeans and the rest of his clothes.

After cleaning up he saw Francesca balled up the linens in piles on the floor. The room smelled like a public bathroom at a dirty nightclub.

Kerrick grabbed his car keys and looked over at her. His heart thick with insensitivity. "You in pain?"

"What do you think, Damien?" she said softly.

He didn't think anything truthfully. If he was being one hundred he didn't give a fuck. He dug into his pocket and grabbed a pack of dope. It was the last of Yori's work and since he wasn't going back, he wanted to unload it on her. He tossed it on the undressed bed.

"What is that?" she asked looking down at the drugs.

"Something to make you feel better."

She stared upon it. Confused. "Are you offering me heroin? When you know what I've been through?"

"You asked for weed when I came over earlier. I don't have any. You can have that if you want it. Either way I'm gone." He bounced toward the door and out of the room.

Fran didn't follow him this time. Instead she dropped to her knees and cried on the floor.

He left the house and was about to go back inside when he heard her crying harder. But it would be a waste of time since he didn't feel for anyone or anybody but himself. Still he wanted to see what type of woman he was dealing with.

He knew she had a history with heroin but had gotten clean. If she avoided the drugs he would treat her better in the future. If not he would continue to use her for his sick pleasures.

Instead of knocking on the door he crept toward the back window that led to her bedroom. The blinds were partially open and he could see Francesca sitting on the bed with her back faced him. At first he thought she was crying, but when he saw a pillow of smoke rise over her head he knew what she was doing. Getting high.

Disappointed, he stepped away from the window. A few branches cracked under his foot as he made his way to the curb. He had his answer. She would never be more than a device he used for his own sick needs. Nothing more. Nothing less.

CHAPTER SIX
KERRICK

"The king's name is a tower of strength."
-William Shakespeare

It was 8:00pm when Kerrick threw the door open in his house. Blood covered his t-shirt and jeans and he was breathing heavily. Anger washed over him.

He had been out all day trying to get a job before things got violent. Things started out normal. He went from one restaurant to another trying to find work as a cook or dishwasher but he had zero luck.

One place acted as if they didn't understand a word he was saying even though when he tried, his accent was unrecognizable. Another diner owner said that he was too black to be seen at night, so they couldn't hire him. He was known for not giving African Americans jobs and had Kerrick known he never would have applied. But the joke was on the owner not Kerrick who waited on him to lock up later that night.

The moment the owner closed his restaurant, with his back turned toward the street, Kerrick cracked a liquor bottle sitting on the curb, so that it produced a jagged edge. Then he rushed up behind him, put his hand on his mouth to silence his cries.

"Surprise, Whitey. You were right, I guess I am too black for you to have seen me at night." Kerrick whispered into his ear before bringing the bottle across his throat, killing him instantly.

After washing up, he sat at the dining room table and rubbed his temples. Victoria came behind him and handed him a glass of vodka. "Drink up, husband. You look like you've had a rough day."

He tossed it back, smiled and pulled her into his lap. She was face to face with him. Looking directly into his large eyes she said, "I don't care what anyone says, you aren't the dishwasher type. So I'm glad you didn't get the job."

Over the years, thanks to dealing with Kerrick she had actually grown wise. And Kerrick was amazed.

"Why do you say that?" he asked curiously. "I'm a man. And a man is supposed to care for his wife."

"You already know what belongs to you, Kerrick," she said calling him by his real name that he finally informed her of recently. She touched his face softly. "And I don't care how long it takes you to get it. Just claim it now. That's the start."

"What are you talking about?" He asked rubbing her white ass.

"Your blocks."

Kerrick sighed. "You don't know what you're talking about. Yori is never going to give it up."

"If he does or doesn't that's on him. But if you ask me you shouldn't waste anymore time."

After all his attempts to pursue a legal lifestyle failed, he went back to the block. Kerrick just finished moving all of his work and was waiting on Yori to bring him more. He had been thinking all night about a plan that would show Abraham that he was more capable than his minion.

The answer came to him when he saw the other foot soldiers playing and joking on the job. There were three of them. Mox, Riley and Jameson and they all were shabby businessmen.

Mox, a pudgy kid, made it known that the only reason he sold drugs was to have enough money to stuff his fat face. His neck was always sweating no matter the weather and his voice was raspy and low as if he were whispering.

Since he was the worst, Kerrick decided to start with him.

So he padded toward Mox who was sitting on the step eating a bowl of chili from a carryout up the block. One of the reasons Kerrick outsold the men was because the three of them were lazier than a newborn baby. Mox was no exception.

"You plan on working today?" Kerrick asked as if he were his boss.

"Fuck you worried about it for, African?" Mox asked stuffing a spoonful of food in his mouth.

Irritated Kerrick slapped the cup out of his hand and watched the food splatter against the grungy ground.

"Fuck is wrong with you?" Mox yelled as he jumped up preparing to challenge him.

But when he realized that Kerrick stood as tall as a Baltimore city lamppost he backed down. Besides, Kerrick's reputation preceded him and Mox preferred his beef in his food not his life.

"Get back to work," Kerrick responded as if he were boss. "The days of fucking around are over."

With Mox under control, a few days later he decided it was time to approach Riley. Riley was older than everyone else on the block but he was the biggest shit starter of the crew. He was more interested in neighborhood gossip than he was moving a pack and stacking bread. He was worse than a bitch with his gossip game. It was because of him that Chill was killed because he was working the block by himself when Riley was supposed to be with him.

Riley was also the cause of a recent beef they had on the streets. An East Baltimore crew came over and sprayed everything standing with bullets. Luckily nobody got hit but had Riley not disrespected one of the gang member's mothers by saying he saw her giving a blow job to a dealer for dope, the event would not have happened in the first place.

When Kerrick decided to get him in shape Riley was standing against the building talking to a cute chick with a fat ass. "Riley, you must not want to make money," he said walking up on them.

Riley looked away from the woman he was planning to sex in the alley and focused on Kerrick. "Fuck you say to me, African?"

"I said you must not want to make money. Everyday you out here rapping some bitch up instead of helping the squad. So I want to know if you out here for paper or not."

Riley left his lady friend and stepped toward Kerrick. He didn't get a chance to check him because suddenly his face was stinging. When he touched his cheek he felt thick warm liquid. It was blood. He didn't even see Kerrick gash him. How did he move so quickly?

The girl Riley was keeping time with bolted up the block to save her own life. He wasn't her man anyway. He was too fucking cheap.

Riley's eyes widened and he yelled, "You cut me!"

"You won't need more than two to three stitches. But if you desire, I can give you something a little wider to complain about." Kerrick reached out his finger, touched the wound and looked at the blood. He rubbed it on Riley's shirt and said, "What's it gonna be? I ain't got all day."

"Can I…I mean…can I at least clean my face first?" Riley asked.

"Make it quick."

Needless to say neither Riley nor Mox caused him any more problems. His next conquest was Jameson. But this situation was different. Kerrick actually liked Jameson and respected him. He felt that if Riley or Mox weren't frolicking on the job that Jameson would have taken his duties more seriously. So instead of approaching him at all Kerrick elected to wait. He waited until sales went up and the business got respectful. He waited until Jameson could see the other two taking things more seriously. And two weeks later as Kerrick predicted Jameson came to him.

Jameson was a tall ex-high school basketball star who injured himself on a layup and lost his career. Not being able to tolerate college without a career in ball, he took to the streets instead. Besides, he'd gotten use to the idea of having money and he couldn't go back. He already nourished his dreams. He and Kerrick had similar pasts in that regard.

Kerrick was standing against the building watching the operation run smoothly when Jameson walked up. "Say man, you wanna grab a drink later?" Jameson asked. "I'm thinking about going to the pool hall."

"I don't see why not," Kerrick responded as if he didn't care either which way. Actually he could've used the male companionship. He hadn't had it since he left Zimbabwe.

"So I'll meet you at the Hall on Liberty Road later tonight." Jameson took a few steps but stopped short. "Oh...and I 'ppreciate you getting shit straight around here. If we got hit for our stash again I had plans to start my own gig. So whatever you need to keep shit smooth let me know."

CHAPTER SEVEN

KERRICK

SEPTEMBER - 1976

"Talkers are no good doers."
-William Shakespeare

Years had passed and the only thing that changed in Kerrick's life was that he was a father.

He wasn't worried about rushing. He knew that in time his plan would come together. Besides, under Kerrick's supervision, Yori's crew had grown very profitable. More dope flooded the blocks and they needed more soldiers to work them. On the streets they were calling Kerrick Mr. Profit.

On the low Yori rewarded Kerrick for managing the men by giving him a few more points on the package. But Kerrick wanted what he always did, to meet the real boss in person. Every other day Yori would promise a meeting but every time the day came he would make excuses or be nowhere to be found. Kerrick was getting frustrated and it took everything he had not to attack.

Truth be told, Yori had no intention on connecting Kerrick with Abraham. Why would he? In the Boss's eyes Yori was doing a good job and he loved the extra attention. He knew that if Abraham caught wind that Kerrick was responsible for the economic growth, he would be reporting to Kerrick instead.

Even Jameson talked to Kerrick about the matter over drinks. As time went by he and Jameson had gotten closer. Their bond was solidified when he learned that Jameson's family was from Nigeria. Before long Jameson had not only become a co-worker but a close friend.

When Kerrick expressed how Yori was playing him soft, Jameson suggested he not work so hard for him anymore. He said to let the operation fall so that Yori would have to keep his promise to set up the meeting. But the worker in Kerrick couldn't see slacking. Instead with each passing day he grew bitter, until he had so much hate in his heart for Yori that it bubbled to the surface and showed in his attitude.

He was standing on the block considering the many ways he wanted to crush Yori when Francesca stomped up the block. She had been blowing up his phone for two months straight but he never returned her calls. She decided she wasn't going to wait anymore and took things into her own hands.

Kerrick wasn't trying to ignore her on purpose. He didn't care about the drug addicted bitch either which way. Besides, after getting off the block he would go home to his wife and help care for their baby so that she would have a break. But Fran didn't want to hear it. All she knew was that she wanted him to spend more time with her.

Kerrick was from Africa, where women stayed in their place and he didn't see why now should be any different. That went for his wife too. The last time Victoria talked slick after an argument he put her out of her own house for a month. And she was seven months pregnant at the time.

When Fran walked up on him he was disgusted. Ever since he turned her back on heroin her body was frail and her clothes were not as fresh as they usually were. Had it not been for her wet mouth and tight asshole he would've left her a long time ago. But he needed someone to take his sexual aggression on when things got rough and Francesca was it.

Fran stuffed her hands in her jacket and said, "Can you please tell me why—"

Her words were halted when Kerrick gripped her by the neck and escorted her to the alley for a little privacy. With her oxygen supply cut off, Francesca's face turned beet red until he released her. Grateful she didn't die, she dropped to her knees and tried to breathe.

He remained unsympathetic as he looked down on her with disdain. "Fuck are you doing around here, Fran?"

She hacked a few times to clear her passageway. When she was getting a little air into her lungs she stood up, leaned against the wall and looked at him with trepidation. "Why haven't you called me?" She asked although the only thing she wanted to do now was run home. She stayed so high that she forgot what kind of monster he could be but now it was too late.

"Because I didn't want to talk to you."

"But I have something important to tell you, Damien."

"What…is…it?" he asked slowly. "And make it quick."

She placed her hand on her lower stomach and said, "I'm pregnant."

A dark cloud seemed to hover over Kerrick's head upon hearing the news. He moved closer to her and she walked backwards into the brick wall where she couldn't move. "What do you mean you're pregnant? You told me you were on the pill."

"I know, baby. But I…I must've missed a day."

She was a liar and he knew it. She would do all she could to have a child by him if it meant keeping him in her life. "You think I'm stupid? Huh? You had to have missed more than one day taking the pill to get pregnant, Fran."

"One or two…it doesn't—"

Kerrick removed a switchblade from his pocket, hit the button and entered her abdomen swiftly. He kept it in place as Fran wiggled to the ground. Her eyes were as wide as her fall. She couldn't believe the man she loved would want to take her life. As he kept the blade in place Kerrick looked over his shoulder to see who was watching. The block was clear so he was good.

When he was satisfied the damage was done he removed the blade, wiped it on her jacket and stood up. "You can't have a baby by me, Fran," he said coldly. "I'm sorry."

Francesca lie in the bed as the hospital machines beeped softly around her. She had spent two days recovering from surgery only for the doctor to tell her what she never wanted to hear as a woman. That she lost her baby and could never have another. The blade Kerrick pressed into her abdomen had successfully pierced her uterus and now she was barren.

She turned her head toward the open window and silently wished for death. Daylight spilled inside and burned her eyes but she didn't look away. Tears cruised down her face and dampened the pillow behind her head. All she wanted was a hit. To get high and forget about everything.

Prior to meeting Kerrick she had a life and friends. It may not have been the best life but it was hers, free of drugs and violence. But now nobody dealt with her because all she wanted was to talk about how much she loved Kerrick. She was boring. Her buddies got tired of that shit and left her alone.

After tiring from staring out the window, she turned her head in the opposite direction and Kerrick was standing in the doorway. Worried he was coming back to finish her off, she sat up in the bed to press the nurses button but he stopped her.

"I'm not here to hurt you," he said calmly, as he touched her hand. He was holding a single red rose, which he laid in her lap. "How do you feel?"

Her voice quivered. "You ruined my life, Damien. And then you come in here and ask me how I feel?"

"I'm a married man, Francesca," he said calmly. "And you could never have a child by me. I told you that. It was one of my rules. Remember?"

"But if you didn't want me I could've been with someone else!" she yelled. "I could've had a family of my own! Now it's because of you that I'm unable to have kids and I could've died."

"Francesca, you would not have died. I have gutted many women like that and they have all survived after losing their babies. I'm a surgeon in that regard. I pierced you exactly where I needed to. Directly in your uterus. And as far as you having children of your own I need to be clear. You will never have another man outside of me," he said seriously. "I'm the last man you will ever be with so get use to it."

Fear enveloped her. "What…what do you mean?"

"I was clear. You and I both know that."

She sobbed uncontrollably. "What makes you think I'm going to be with you after what you've done? Huh? What makes you think I won't move far away if I must just to get away from you?"

"Because you're an addict," he placed a tuff of her hair behind her ear. "And you will always be an addict. I'm the only one in this world who will give you a free supply. And, if you ever got clean and tried to leave me, I will hunt you down and kill you."

"But why won't you just let me go? If you don't love me and won't make me your wife?"

"Love is so overrated. What you and I have is better. It's an arrangement." He walked to the head of the bed and kissed her on the forehead. "Now get well. I hate hospitals. They're always so cold."

CHAPTER EIGHT

1981

5 YEARS LATER

"There is something in the wind."
-William Shakespeare

It seemed like the more things changed the more they stayed the same in Kerrick's life. After five years he had five children and no more power on the streets. His commitment to being a great employee crippled him, and forced him to remain under Yori's command. Although he had gotten more money and a little more control over the soldiers, it wasn't enough. The blocks did run smoother because he was in charge. But he wanted full control. He wanted full power.

He felt that Yori wasn't taking him seriously because he was African. They always joked about his slight accent and color of his skin. One of his favorite moments was when they rented out the strip club and his white wife showed up. She was so beautiful that no one could take their eyes off of her, not even Yori. It was the only time he'd gotten respect but he was sure that it wouldn't be his last.

After a long day's work Kerrick stormed into the house and threw his coat on the couch. His wife was in the recliner watching TV and three of their children were sitting at her feet. The older children, five-year-old Kelly and four-year-old Avery were somewhere else in the house.

When Kerrick's family saw the stone faced expression he wore they didn't bother to greet him. They knew the leader of their family well enough and knew when to back off.

"Children, go to your rooms," Victoria told the pack quietly. When they were gone she addressed her husband carefully. "Honey, can I make you a drink?" She asked considering his foul mood. "Or something to eat?"

"Gin. No food," he responded coldly.

She rushed to make his drink and returned it to him. He was sitting on the sofa and his right leg shook as he tried to calm down.

Victoria pinched her neck a few times out of nervousness, causing red lesions. "Can I take care of you?" She asked softly.

He sat his cup down and undid his jeans. Victoria crawled between his legs, removed his penis and gave him a sloppy wet blowjob. He didn't have a dry place on his dick when she was done.

The moment he released his semen into her throat he looked down at her. She smiled and said, "Yori has to die." She placed his dick back into his jeans and sat on his lap.

"It's not that easy, Victoria."

She kissed his right cheek and then his left. "Why isn't it? For the last six months you have been beside yourself with anger. A king can't remain under a peasant for long." She placed a warm hand on his face. "You have the soldiers, Kerrick. So you have the blocks. Take them. I'm begging you."

"It won't be easy."

"Taking over a kingdom seldom is."

After a long shower, Kerrick sat in the living room and thought about what his wife said. She was right. It was time to attack. His only dilemma was how.

He was about to go to bed when he heard some giggling in the den. Since all of the children were supposed to be in bed he was confused. When he opened the door he saw his two oldest children sitting on the floor kissing each other.

At first he was about to rush in and shake them to death for acting on their emotions. And then he looked at them. Their light skin…a product of himself and his beautiful white wife. They were perfect. So it was natural for them to be attracted to each other. They lived in a country without code or honor. Their father on the other hand was born in Africa and as a result his blood was close to royalty. So he closed the door and left them alone. He would be back for them later to be sure they went to bed.

Slowly he walked into his room, not sure what he was actually saying. It didn't take him long to make a decision. He did not want his children breeding with African Americans. He wanted them to breed amongst themselves and stay pure.

With his mind made up he crawled into bed with his wife. At first he wasn't going to tell her about what he saw, but he wanted to prepare her for his future plan. "I saw Avery and Kelly in the den."

"What were they doing?" she asked with suspicious eyes. Her demeanor told him that what they shared they had done before.

"Kissing."

"I'm sorry, Kerrick. I don't know what has gotten into them lately. I think it's because you don't want them to go to a public school. They don't have any friends outside of themselves and it may be a bad idea. They are spending too much time with one another."

He frowned. "I told you I don't want my children around these American niggers. Their minds will be corrupted and I won't have that! Continue to home school them. And if you need help I'll get you someone. But they must remain in this house. My family is all I have and I don't want them altered." He looked into her eyes and he looked like a demon. "I have a plan that will keep my bloodline pure and you may not like it but you will have to trust me."

"Are you saying what I think you are?" she looked over at him hoping he wasn't implying incest would be their way of life.

"I married you because you agreed to follow my lead. I hope I didn't make a mistake."

It had been two weeks since Kerrick decided to relinquish power over the soldiers and it was difficult. In order for his plan to work, he decided to slack off too. Because he was always up early, he would have to find something to do just to be late for work. He was determined to stop doing Yori's dirty work. If he wanted to rule the blocks and take the credit, Kerrick would give them to him.

The first week the profits went down and the workers weren't pumping as hard. Yori asked Kerrick if everything was cool and he always said yes. Yori assumed it was a bad week or that a rival gang had released free dope testers, which caused them to have low business. But for damage control he promised to introduce Kerrick to Abraham just to be sure. But Kerrick wasn't playing the game anymore. He would simply nod and walk off.

When sales dropped the second week Yori got his ass handed to him by Abraham. His job was threatened along with his life so he had to make a move.

Without Kerrick placing the fear of God into the men, things weren't as smooth as a Bentley engine anymore. Yori realized he had a long run of taking responsibility for Kerrick's work and now it was time to render to Cesar.

"Have you been noticing anything weird with the soldiers?" Yori asked Kerrick.

"Naw," he said looking up and down the block for a customer. "I just do me."

"I know. Your money is always right," he responded. "But what about everyone else?"

When Yori looked over at Riley, Mox and Jameson, he grew angry. Riley was standing in the cut entertaining a cute dark skin girl with a large ass and a bright smile. Mox was eating a hot dog from 7-Eleven while another sat in his lap. Even Jameson was tripping as he held a large gray cell phone to his ear.

Realizing the men only respected him if Kerrick was in control Yori asked, "What do you want, Damien?"

Kerrick acted as if he had no idea what he was talking about. "You gotta be clearer, man."

Yori exhaled. "You want to meet Abraham? Is that what you want?"

"I want you to be a man and keep your promise."

Yori shuffled a little. "Okay. You got that. But first I want you to go with me to pick up a shipment that's being delivered tomorrow. When that business is done I'll introduce you to Abraham."

Kerrick remained planted, not sure if he should believe him or not. "You should know that if you lie to me again this time there would be problems for your health."

Yori swallowed hard. "I just want to make money, man," he said, fearing Kerrick more than God. He extended his hand. "Do we have a deal?"

Kerrick looked at his grubby little fingers. The last time he thought he had a deal with him he was left on the block for five years. So he took his time excepting his offer. He wanted Yori to feel like he was dealing with his boss instead of his subordinate. When he was ready, he shook Yori's hand firmly, squeezing his fingers in the process.

Then he snapped his finger and all of the soldiers fell in line.

Riley sent the bitch about her business. Mox threw his hot dog in the trash and Jameson stuffed the huge phone, which he wasn't talking on anyway, in his baggy acid washed jean pocket.

Yori looked at his soldiers. His mouth fell open and his bottom lip trembled. The level of disrespect his senior men exhibited had him thinking about retiring. "So…they…they were in on this the entire time?"

Kerrick winked and walked away.

Not even the night sky could hide the shape of the building Kerrick followed Yori into. If anybody wanted to display an act of kindness, using a couple of blocks of C4 to blow the bitch up, would've sufficed.

The hairs on the back of Kerrick's neck rose as he walked into the abandoned tenement. The hallway, flanked on each side with apartments, was dark and dank. After what felt like forever Yori eventually walked to the final unit on the left hand side and opened the door…without a key.

In the middle of the room sat an old wooden table that rocked as they brushed past it to enter. The place didn't seem safe or secure as far as Kerrick was concerned. Whether Yori was being irresponsible or unprofessional to choose a place like that to handle the business didn't matter. Kerrick lost even more respect for him.

"What's up with this place?" Kerrick asked looking up at the ceiling, which was speckled with mold spots. "You do business here for real?" his hands fell by his sides where his .45 rested in his coat pocket. And if things got too fantastic, Jameson and the other men were only a stones throw away outside of the building, waiting on his word.

"What do you think?" Yori said, growing tired of Kerrick's insubordination. "Of course I do business here."

He frowned. "Abraham doesn't know about this deal does he?"

"You tell me everything you do?" Yori responded with disdain. "It's like this, after I introduce you to Abraham I know I'm out of business. So this dope is gonna be for my side gig. And I asked you here to cut you in."

"Why?"

"Why what?" Yori asked taking the money out of the duffle bag and placing it on the table.

"Why must you be so disloyal?" The fire in his words was strong enough to singe Yori's skin.

"Disloyal?" he screamed. "Do you know how long I've walked in Abraham's shadows?" His eyes protruded from the sockets, as he got excited. "How long I did his dirty work, only for him to give me a few scraps like I was a losing pit-bull in a fight?" His voice quivered and he lost all control.

"Was it longer than what you did to me?" Kerrick's response was flat but deserved attention.

"Damien, you have—"

"Kerrick. My name is Kerrick Khumalo and I'm from Zimbabwe."

Damien's entire disposition changed. "So all this time you told me a lie? About who you were? What else don't I know about you?"

"You didn't deserve the truth. Just like you don't deserve a life."

Kerrick removed his weapon and fired once into Yori's skull. His body fell backwards and slammed into the table, breaking it in two. The money fell on his chest and blood mixed with bone matter sat on the top of Kerrick's Super Timberland boot. He kicked it off and it smacked to the floor.

As he watched Yori's corpse lay flat, he had no emotion.

Kerrick walked over to Yori's pocket and removed a bulky cell phone. He scrolled through the phonebook and looked for the most obscure number. When he found the letter "A" he dialed it and a second later Abraham was on the phone.

"This is Damien. I'm calling because I have a package for you that you'll want to receive."

An hour later Abraham went to the address Kerrick had given him. Six men, four with assault weapons aimed in his direction, covered him.

But Kerrick wasn't alone either. Riley, Mox and Jameson stood behind him and all were prepared to give their lives.

When Abraham saw Yori, his oldest soldier, sprawled out on the floor covered in his own blood he looked to Kerrick for an answer.

"You call me here for this?" Abraham barked.

"I did," he responded calmly.

"If you wanted to commit suicide there are easier ways you know."

Kerrick eyed Abraham's armed men. "I know you're a smart man, Abraham," Kerrick said unafraid to die. "But we both know that this man was no good. He lacked both the ambition and leadership needed to run your organization. But I don't. I have every skill necessary but I could no longer work under him. I have no respect for him and neither do his soldiers."

Abraham crossed his arms over his chest and looked at the three men standing behind him. He gnawed the inside of his lip like he'd done in the past, which is why half of the inside of his mouth was gone. "You're the one who sliced the boy up in Mama's Kitchen aren't you?"

"I am."

"And you're the reason for the profit rise."

Kerrick nodded.

Abraham laughed softly. "I was waiting for you to make a move." He paused. "I know men like you. Men like you will do all they can to follow the rules. It took years for you to approach me despite this fucker's horrible work ethic." He nodded as if he had it figured all out. "Your loyalty wouldn't allow you to step to me on your own even though you could've ended this a long time ago."

"You're right on some things. I am loyal but it was never to Yori."

Confused he asked, "Then who was it to?"

"My cause. Loyalty to myself would not allow me to break even though I knew I was a better man than him."

Abraham shook his head upon understanding. Finally he stepped closer to Kerrick. "You're a patient man. And in a world full of hotheads that's refreshing. So I'm going to give you an opportunity. You'll take over Yori's spot. So tell me. What are your conditions?"

Kerrick took a moment to consider what he wanted. Lately whenever his name came up, the word 'profit' did too. Although he liked the name, he decided to change it up slightly.

"I only have two conditions. One is that you call me by my native name…Kerrick." He paused. "Kerrick Prophet."

Abraham grinned loving his response. "With a name like that I can tell we're going to make a lot of money together."

"You're right," Kerrick responded. "And my second condition is that you don't cross me too."

PART TWO

BY T. STYLES

CHAPTER NINE
PRESENT DAY
WINTER, BALTIMORE, MD

PENN STATION

"Extreme fear can neither fight nor fly."
-William Shakespeare

The Predator observed Butterfly through narrow eyes after she recanted the story she knew about her grandfather's life. She wanted her to know that there was a reason for everything she did. Just like there was a reason she tracked her down with the intent to kill her.

"If he was so horrible why are you so much like him?" Butterfly asked.

The Predator looked at her with a blank and emotionless face. "You think I'm like him?" she pointed to herself. "Even more than you?"

"I'm sorry. I made a mistake and I ran when I found out I was pregnant. So much time passed that I thought you had forgotten about me. Until I saw you in the hospital that day holding my baby. I ran because I was trying to survive. Don't you get that?"

The Predator laughed heartedly. "You talk about survival but you know nothing about it. You don't know what it's like to desire to eat and not be fed. You don't know what its like to live in complete darkness while begging for a spark of light. And you don't know what it's like to fear." She sat back and looked at the baby in her arms. "Until now."

"Please…I'm begging you. Don't hurt me. Don't hurt my child."

"You are asking what is not yours. Whatever happens to you tonight, on this train or off it, is my decision alone."

Butterfly's muscles tensed and her breath felt caught inside of her chest. "Yes what I did was wrong. And I'm not proud of it. But you can't sit over there and pretend that your entire life was messed up. Look at you now. You're a Prophet dipped in diamonds and fur. Some people would have died to live in that house."

"It's funny you said that, Butterfly. Because some people did."

CHAPTER TEN

1997

SIXTEEN YEARS LATER

"Make us heirs of all eternity."
-William Shakespeare

The birthing room was warm as Kerrick stood over the bed and watched his twenty-one year old daughter Kelly prepare to bring her third baby into the world. This child, as well as her other two, were by her brother, twenty-year old Avery.

A lot of things changed in sixteen years. For starters the Prophet Family, under Kerrick's rule, had grown to be the most notorious family in DC, Maryland and Virginia. And Victoria had given birth to six children, three of which were girls. Although Kerrick was far from the block boy he started as, he was able to secure a connect in Miami which allowed him access to pure cocaine at better than fair wholesale rate.

He controlled everything and everybody around him. Since secrets surrounded their family, due to most of his grandchildren being a product of inbreeding, he didn't trust many people.

Although Kerrick had many grandchildren, including the two girls named Lydia and Paige that Kelly gave birth too, not one was fairer than his favorite grandchild Alice Prophet. She was born to his third child Marina.

The goal for Kelly was to always have a baby more precious than Alice.

Kerrick was confused. Although he claimed to be proud of being from Africa, over the years he had grown to hate his dark skin and how he was viewed. So he continued to bleach his skin and tried to erase any trace of his heritage. He sold out his own race and was forcing his children to do the same.

"Push, Kelly," Victoria pleaded as she gripped her daughter's left hand while Avery held the other. "Don't stop pushing."

Her light skin reddened as she bore down into the bed to release the child from her body. Puddles of sweat strolled down her forehead as she gave birth with no pain meds, just like all of his daughters. Although Dr. Banning could've given all of Kerrick's girl's medicine to reduce the pain when they went into labor, Kerrick said no. Some said it was because he loved the sound of his daughter's screaming in pain, because it brought him pleasure.

"The baby's head is crowning," Dr. Annette Banning advised. "When you feel the next contraction push again."

Kelly was in habitual dolor with no relief in sight. Still she gripped her brother's hand and squeezed her third baby into the world who she would call Karen.

As the doctor wrapped the baby in a white blanket Kelly could not see her face. So she looked at her father for validation. Was this child perfect? She needed it to be. All of her natural life she did all she could to please him but she always fell short.

Unlike her sisters, all of Kelly's offspring were great disappointments. And every child she bore that he didn't like, she acted as if they didn't exist because it wasn't worth it to have children that her father didn't love.

The doctor's eyes widened as she held the small child in her hand. Something about her expression told Kelly that something was wrong. But since she couldn't see the child she would have to impatiently wait.

After Dr. Banning cleared the baby's passageway it cried loudly. Afterwards she walked Kerrick's 8th grandchild over to him. At first he smiled, hoping that his oldest child would finally get it right. But when the smile vanished and was replaced with disgust tears ran down her face. She fucked up yet again.

Not only was the child nothing like he imagined, due to inbreeding, the baby was severely deformed.

"Father," Kelly asked repositioning herself in the bed. "Is the baby perfect?" she asked hoping that she was reading his expressions incorrectly.

Kerrick frowned and in a rough voice said, "No." He shoved the child into the doctor's arms. "Take it to my daughter." Kerrick's face, which had been bleached harshly over the years, reddened with irritation. He folded his arms over his chest and waited for Kelly to see how she failed.

"What's wrong, father?" Avery asked, afraid for the emotional pain his sister would endure if Kerrick turned his back on her again.

"Don't talk to me," Kerrick pointed at him. "This is your fault too."

Avery, worried he'd be thrown out of the mansion when he couldn't take care of himself, let alone his sister-wife, remained silent.

When the baby was placed in Kelly's arms her hands shook wildly. Slowly she removed the blanket covering the infant's face. And what she saw would haunt her for the rest of her life. The baby was a horrible sight.

Kelly rolled her eyes from the baby, slowly to her father. He was right. She was a worthless daughter who couldn't do anything right. All she wanted was a child Kerrick could frolic around Baltimore so that men young and old would do anything to marry her. The Prophet daughters not only got the proposals, if he allowed them to marry outside the family, they married rich.

Kelly scanned her baby again. It was a girl. Her face was as red as an apple. Her head was luniform shaped and her eyes were not leveled. Huge tears fell out of Kelly's eyes and lines of snot oozed out of her nose. "I'm so sorry, father. Can you ever forgive me?"

Without responding he looked at the doctor. "Dr. Banning, you can leave now."

When the doctor collected her things and exited he focused on his loser daughter. Instead of speaking he used silence as a weapon. Slowly he walked over to Kelly and placed a thick wad of her hair behind her ear.

When he reviewed his grandbaby again it was without emotion. He raised his massive, calloused hand and placed it over the child's face. The infant kicked lightly, about as powerfully as a butterfly under a piece of paper. And then suddenly there was no motion.

Kerrick had murdered his uglified grandchild all because it didn't meet his standard. When his slaying was complete he walked out of the room.

"I'm sorry, Kelly," Victoria cried, unable to control the monster who was her husband. "I'm so sorry about this." She ran out of the room to tend to Kerrick.

A month passed since Kelly had given birth to her child. She was inconsolable although Avery did all he could to appease her.

Since Kelly and Avery were the only children living in the mansion with Kerrick and Victoria, and with him being angry always they avoided him at all costs. Kerrick was already troubled due to his declining drug operation, from not being able to work out arrangements to secure the Baltimore market. The last thing he needed was to see Kelly's pitiful face.

She lie in bed with a box of tissues in her lap. Avery was next to her, rubbing her leg to calm her down. Life as a Prophet was harder than living at a Nazi camp to hear them tell it. He was a dictator and those who were further away from his idea of perfect got it worse.

Living in the Prophet mansion meant keeping a lot of secrets. Because of it they didn't mingle with outsiders unless they earned over two million dollars a year, and had approval by Kerrick. Every one of Kerrick and Victoria's six children were home schooled until they were old enough to attend college so that Kerrick could control who came in and out of their lives.

To date he kept tabs on all of his children, including his estranged son Justin, who was ashamed of the incest that went on in the family and abandoned them. Justin even went as far as to change his last name to Lincoln and he took an outside wife named Corrine. They had one son. Autumn Lincoln.

Kerrick's reason for keeping the family from outsiders was understandable. He was raising a house of horrors. With his approval, to keep his bloodline pure, incest was highly encouraged. So Kelly and Avery had children together. Victory and Blake, also siblings, had four children together. His favorite daughter Marina was allowed to take an outside husband, Joshua Saint, and she had one child.

All of Kerrick's children, with his help and money, were able to make it out in the world. Everyone with the exception of Kelly and Avery. Even with an open wallet they could not live alone. Due to Kelly's declining mental issues the cops were called to whatever house they previously owned repeatedly, and when she was hospitalized she would often mention a few family secrets. So Kerrick decided to take care of them, and he despised them for it too.

"I hate to see you like this," Avery said to his sister wife as he consoled her after not being able to have the perfect child.

"And I'm sorry you have to go through this with me," she said as she faced him with red, swollen eyes. "I know it's hard and your patience is amazing." She placed her hand on the side of his face. "It's just that I don't know what he needs. All I want is for him to love me."

Avery sighed. "I don't know, baby. Maybe we try too hard to please him. Have you ever considered letting it go?"

She spun her head toward him and covered her mouth. "Don't say that," she whispered. "Don't ever talk like that again." Her voice grew louder. "I love father and I know if I could just get this one thing right, he'll love me in return." Her head lowered. "I don't mean to yell but he's all I got."

This panged Avery's heart because through it all he had never left her side. From the day Kerrick caught them kissing in the den as kids until that moment he had dedicated his life to her. Yet nobody meant more to her than Kerrick and Avery resented his father because of it.

Before he could respond their children Lydia and Paige walked into the room. They were six-year old Irish Twins who lived in the mansion with them. The moment Kelly saw the fuck ups she gave birth to she grew disgusted. They were dirty and fat, and she accepted zero responsibility for the children's filthy upkeep. In her mind it was all their faults.

Because she didn't love them, they were allowed to eat what they wanted and do what they wanted just as long as they stayed away from her. To that day neither Kelly or Avery had ever hugged their children.

Lydia's huge stomach protruded from the red t-shirt she wore and the large black sweatpants were stained with mustard. Although her face was cute, she was born fat and grew more obese as the years went by. The saddest part was that Lydia was severely attention starved.

Because she didn't receive affection from her parents, she used food to compensate for her feelings. There had been so many times when she asked for hugs from her mother, only for Kelly to be preoccupied with her own emotions and feelings. Avery would at least smile at them if he had a moment, before warning his daughters to stay out of his way.

Paige was much shorter than her sister but slightly more attractive. The white night gown she always wore drowned out her body and was stained with mustard; also from the raw hot dogs they ate earlier.

Unlike her sister, Paige handled her need for attention in other ways. She ignored her parents and pretended they didn't exist. When the pain of not being loved hit her she took to cutting her hair, leaving bald spots scattered throughout her scalp in the process.

Paige had another problem that made Kerrick angry. Although inbreeding was accepted, he frowned upon homosexuality. Paige had been caught several times touching her sister and cousins the wrong way, and most ran when they saw her coming.

Poor Paige and Lydia. In a family full of awkward people, they were the weirdest. And that made life hard.

"Mama, can I get in the bed with you?" Lydia asked as Paige flopped at the foot of the bed, with her back turned toward them. She played with the edge of her nightgown but could hear the entire conversation.

"I don't want to be bothered right now," Kelly yelled, blowing her nose into the napkin. "Take your sister and go outside somewhere. Every time I turn around you're in my face. Give me a moment's peace. Please!"

She could feel her eyes watering, which always happened when her mother hurt her feelings. "Well can you come outside with me?" Lydia asked with hopeful eyes. "Maybe we can water grandfather's plants."

"Honey, your mother doesn't feel well," Avery announced. "And you know you shouldn't be touching your grandfather's things. Now go play in your room. Maybe I'll read a bedtime story to you later," he lied.

Lydia knew that lie all too well. Avery promised both girls on many occasions that he'd read them a bedtime story but he never came.

"Okay," Lydia said with a smile. "But can mama watch me play out of the window?"

"I said your mother doesn't feel good," Avery yelled.

"She never feels good," Paige interrupted with disdain in her voice, as she tugged at the threads on the edge of her gown.

"Mind your mouth," Avery said as he rose up to observe his daughter sitting on the floor. All he could see was the top of her splotchy head. "Now go outside, both of you, and leave your mother be."

Irritated by her parents, Paige jumped up and stomped toward her room, leaving her sister alone. She didn't want to see her parents anyway but Lydia begged her to go with her.

"Can I sit over there then?" Lydia asked pointing to the beautiful daybed by the window. "On the bed? I promise not to talk."

Avery shook his head. If he could say anything about his child it was that she was persistent.

"Damn it, Lydia," Kelly yelled. "Why can't you just go play by yourself? I said I'm not in the mood. Now leave me be!"

Lydia rocked back and forth as she stood on her mother's side of the bed. Her toes curled under and she tried to think of something cute to say, like she did when she was younger, and made her mother smile. So she spun around in place and did a dance she practiced last week with her sister. Her arms flailed at her sides as she performed for her parents' love.

"Lydia, stop the stupidness," Kelly screamed. "I'm not going to tell you again! Get out of here! I wish you were never born!"

Lydia stopped in place and froze all movements. She gazed into her mother's eyes, hoping she would reach for her and say she was sorry. It never happened.

Defeated she fulfilled her parents wishes, leaving them both alone.

"Don't worry about her, baby," Avery said rubbing Kelly's shoulder. "She'll be okay."

"I don't understand why she doesn't see that I'm in emotional pain," Kelly whined. "That I'm hurting. All she cares about is her own fat self. Father is right, we do have horrible children."

"She's a child and if you ask me we spoiled them rotten. Both of them. I should've showed them their baby sister before we buried her so that they could see what could've happened to them. If you ask me they should be grateful."

Kelly looked into her brother-husband's eyes. "I love you so much, Avery. Please don't ever leave me."

"That's impossible. You're my world, baby."

They were about to make love when they heard loud screaming in the larger part of the house. Both of them hopped out of bed and ran toward the voice. It was their mother. And she was standing in the foyer holding her bloodied grandchild Lydia in her arms.

Kelly's eyes widened and her jaw dropped. She didn't understand what she was looking at. "Who is that?" she trembled while pointing at the bloodied body.

"It's Lydia," Victoria sobbed.

Kelly looked at Avery and then back at her mother. "She's not dead." Kelly tried to tell herself. "She's just fighting for attention." She snatched her child from her mother and shook her roughly. "Wake up. Wake up, and stop being a brat." Lydia's body vibrated like a ragdoll in her hand and her eyes never opened. "I'll play with you if you stop playing."

In the corner Paige stood with her fist stuffed in her mouth, to mute her cries. She lost the only person who cared if she got up every morning. And she hated her parents deeply now.

Avery took Lydia from Kelly and tried to do CPR. Kelly looked down at him, still stuck and confused.

"What happened?" Kelly asked her mother as her body convulsed.

"She ran out into the highway and was hit by a car," Victoria sobbed, wiping her tears away with her diamond-studded hand.

After the CPR appeared in vein, Avery placed a finger on the vein on her neck. He didn't detect movement. "Oh my, God, honey. She's dead."

When Lydia was killed Kelly milked the attention from her parents. Although Kerrick didn't care for Kelly's children, he didn't want them dead either, especially if it took place in front of their home. So he tolerated giving her a hug or two and they were allowed to eat dinner at the dining room table with him, just as long as they remained silent.

Still there was the problem with Lydia's death. To avoid attention and keep their family's secrecy, Kerrick buried his grandchild in the acres of land, which covered his property. Although his children didn't understand that sex amongst siblings was against the law, he knew the truth. He also knew that Lydia's death could've caused problems if detectives started snooping around asking questions.

To make sure he covered his tracks, Kerrick tracked down the drunk driver who ran away from the scene. When he did he had his pregnant wife killed and told him that if he ever came forward he would murder him too. He let him stay alive so that he would remember everyday that it was because he killed his grandchild that he would not see his seed grow.

And then there was his other granddaughter Paige who ran away from home. He did all he could do to find her but she vanished. This sent Kelly further over the edge.

To keep Kelly from not losing her mind, Kerrick gave her access to more money and allowed her to use his favorite car, his silver Porsche. But after awhile he grew tired of her weak spirit and put her back in the doghouse. He wouldn't talk to her as much. Told her to stay away when he ate his dinner. It was as if she didn't exist. It was at this time that she announced that she was pregnant again.

Although Kelly boasted over and over how the baby growing in her belly would make Kerrick proud he never believed her. The only thing he wanted was for his daughter to get a life and leave him alone.

On January 1st 1998, the day Kelly felt contractions, Victoria contacted the doctor. As usual Kerrick, Victoria, Dr. Annette Banning and Avery were present.

Kelly's vanilla colored legs were placed in cold metal stirrups and spread open. Her entire body trembled with pain due to not having meds. Victoria took her daughter's right hand to calm her down while Avery grabbed the left. She had an extreme urge to shit and the doctor knew it was time.

The Dr. placed a latex glove on, widened Kelly's legs and entered her vagina until she felt the opening of her cervix. "You're dilated." She said with a smile. "It's time. Are you ready?"

Kelly nodded. "I think so."

"Okay, when you feel the next contraction push."

Kelly looked over at her father who stood across the room. "I'm going to have a baby you'll love as much as Alice, father. If not more. I promise you."

Kerrick remained in the corner with his arms crossed over his chest. He wasn't interested in this spectacle in the least. The only reason he was present was to make sure nobody said the wrong thing in front of the outsider in his home. Because although she was the doctor she had no idea that the woman on the bed and the man to her right were siblings.

"Push," the doctor encouraged.

"You can do it, honey," Avery said softly. "I love you so much."

Kelly pushed harder until finally a baby slid out. Dr. Banning grabbed the sheet, covered the child and cleared its airways. When it cried she smiled. As with the others she walked it over to Kerrick and he looked down at it. This was the moment of truth. The only moment that mattered to Kelly.

Kelly and Avery observed Kerrick's expression. They were hopeful that this child would be what he deemed beautiful. Which meant high yellow skin, and beautiful thin features. But when he looked over at her and frowned her heart broke yet again. "Get this child out of my face," he scoffed.

Sadly the Dr. walked the baby over to Kelly as she did before and placed it in her arms. Since her work was done she said her goodbyes, gathered her things and left the property. She was always stressed when coming to the Prophet home. Things always seemed tense.

Huge tears rolled down Kelly's face even though she had not seen the child. It didn't matter what she thought anyway. If Kerrick wasn't going to be happy with the baby, neither would she.

Still, Kelly took a deep breath and removed the cover to see the child's face. She was pleasantly surprised. A quick smile appeared before disappearing at once. After all, this baby was different. It was a girl. Her nose was thin, her cheeks were rosy and she was…well…beautiful. But, and this was the most important thing, her skin was as brown as the bark on a tree.

Kerrick walked over to his daughter and looked down at her. "And you disappoint me again."

"Kerrick, please don't do this," Victoria said. "It isn't her fault that her children are not to your liking."

He threw his wife an evil stare that forced her out of the room. Although she wanted to be there for her children she had no power when it came to her husband. He had become a monster. And yet he remained her master.

Kerrick focused his attention back to his daughter. He raised his hand like he had before and placed a strand of her hair behind her ear. Afterwards he removed his hand and placed it over the infant's face. He was not about to take care of another one of his daughter's fuck ups.

"Father, please don't do this," Avery whispered. "It's my baby."

Kerrick slapped him with the back of his hand, slicing his bottom lip open. He fell to the floor where he remained.

Ignoring his son and daughter he continued to push down on the baby's face until Kelly said, "Daddy, please…I lost Lydia; and Paige has vanished. I don't want to lose another child. I promise you, you will never know she's in the house if you let me keep her."

Kerrick continued to press the baby's face with his hand to snuff out its life.

"I'll even stay out of your way," she continued. "And I won't bother you again or try to have another child."

With that promise he slowly raised his hand. He would give anything if he didn't have to be bothered with her or her unworthy pregnancies. But when he looked down at the child, its eyes were closed. She looked dead. Thinking that the deal he made with his daughter wouldn't matter anyway, he was preparing to walk out of the room, leaving them with the responsibility of burying her out back with the rest.

And then the baby gasped and her limbs jerked wildly as she cried out. Kelly sobbed and laughed at the same time. "She's alive. Oh my, god, she's alive."

Kerrick was impressed with the child's strength. But it was not attractive enough to be a Prophet. "This child will not have a family name," he told her. "You will simply call her *Nine*. Because she is the ninth grandchild."

"Okay, father," Kelly nodded wiping her tears away. "Okay."

"And you will remember the promise you gave to me. I don't want to ever be bothered with you again. And I'm going to schedule you an appointment for Dr. Banning to cut your tubes. Clear?"

Kelly nodded as she realized all of the hopes she had to make him proud by having the perfect child were gone. “Clear.”

Kerrick exited the birthing room.

Avery stood up and wiped the blood off of his bottom lip with the cuff of his button down white shirt. He walked over to his wife and looked down at the dark and beautiful child in her arms. “What made you give up fighting for his love? It’s what you want more than anything.”

She wiped the tears from her face. “I don’t know, Avery.” She looked down at Nine. “I don’t know. But something in my heart tells me she’s worth it. I can feel it.”

CHAPTER ELEVEN

16 YEARS LATER

2014

"As quiet as a lamb."
-William Shakespeare

Kerrick sat at a large cherry wood dining room table with Johnny Gates, who ran Baltimore City, sitting on the other side. The vaulted roof was interrupted with beautiful windows that caused light to bounce off the table making the expensive China and silverware sparkle.

Victoria, who cooked because the family maid had been gone for three days, prepared a delicious Latin American meal and now the men were full. It was time to discuss business.

"So, Gates, now that you have been properly courted," Kerrick chuckled, "Can you tell me if you are willing to use my product in Baltimore?"

"You want to discuss this now? At a time like this?"

"What better time? Your belly is full right?"

Johnny Gates was a fifty-seven year old man who had been in the drug business longer than he cared to admit. Although he was rich, he was smart and kept his purchases and finances low.

His father, Billy Gates, was the biggest dealer Houston had ever seen. But he had a penchant for pussy and even indulged himself with his best friend's wife, which caused him to be hung by his neck for all his men to see.

So Johnny, who was twenty at the time, took the money his father stashed at the house, along with his knowledge of the business to Baltimore city. There he met Abraham, and supplied him heroin using his father's connect.

Business was good. That is until Abraham's neck was slit at his ten year old son's football game. At first no one knew he was dead. His lifeless stare was taken as a lack of enthusiasm since his kid's team was losing. But when the game was over and his son walked into the bleachers and touched him, his body fell on his son. Then everyone had become aware, Kerrick had killed him.

The reason for the hit was known to most. Kerrick had gained the trust of a Miami Drug Cartel and they supplied him with pure cocaine. Abraham refused to use his product and paid with his life. Although Kerrick still didn't supply Baltimore, because Johnny Gates, a made man, was next in charge, Kerrick's reputation for ruthlessness was legendary. Which is why Gates never trusted him.

Kerrick was going to kill Gates too but men he trusted warned him against it. They said that if he made a move without authorization his entire family would be annihilated. Kerrick was going to take his chances anyway until Gates made a classy move first.

Gates invited Kerrick to a luxurious cigar bar outside of Baltimore. And over expensive smokes and whisky, he respectfully declined his offer to use his product. His tactfulness was the only reason Kerrick let him live. Everybody else who bucked against his system was buried along with close family members and friends.

After awhile Gates grew interesting to Kerrick. He was a man who got everything but he couldn't get Gates to relent. Gates was a challenge. The more he said no the more Kerrick trusted him, which was why he invited him to his home. Gates had proven that he wasn't a man of circumstance, but integrity, something that he couldn't say for himself.

In one way they were alike. They had big families. Gates had three daughters, a set of twins and a seventeen year old. And Kerrick had his six children.

"Where are your manners?" Gates asked playfully as he rubbed his salt and pepper beard again. "You haven't even offered me a glass of your best. Yet you speak to me about business?"

Kerrick grinned. "You're right. I'll grab the bottle. It's on the kitchen counter."

"No," Gates pushed back in the chair. "Please allow me."

"It's fine with me, it's behind you to the right," Kerrick responded.

Gates stood up and made his way toward the dark kitchen. With each step he took he was trying to find a creative way of saying no. But his thoughts disappeared into the ether when he saw an open refrigerator with a naked woman standing in front of it.

Her back was in his direction and he was mesmerized as he watched her stuff food in her mouth by the handfuls. She was so preoccupied that she didn't know Gates was present. But he saw her and couldn't help but admire her sexy physique.

The light from the open fridge seemed to make her chocolate skin effervescent. Her slender back led to her plump ass which extended as if it had a mind of it's own. Her legs were thick but far from fat and only added to her appeal. She was alluring.

When she turned her head slightly to the side he caught the silhouette of her profile. Her lips were plump and pink and her nose was slender and perfect. At that point Gates had several questions. Who was the scavenger? And why was she naked?

He was still enamored until he saw the faint discoloration of scars on her back. They resembled small tree branches which extended outward. Was she being beaten?

"I know my house is big but you didn't get that lost did you," Kerrick asked cheerfully until he walked up on Gates and saw who held his attention.

When Kerrick saw Nine's nude body he stopped in mid stride and his eyes bulged. At first he was speechless as he watched his associate observe his secret. This type of thing could get into the streets and cause problems. He considered killing Gates right there but in the past Gates had proven to be a man of honor. So he would think of another way to clean up the issue.

Kerrick rushed into the kitchen, grabbed a hand towel off the stove and placed it over Nine's plump rear.

Nine was startled and said, "Grandfather, I'm so sorry." Her eyes widened with fear. She wasn't supposed to be out of her room. She was scared but the need to survive trumped any future outcomes. "I was hungry and didn't mean to—,"

"Don't worry about that," he said smiling at Gates. "Victoria, get down here!" he yelled. "Now!"

A few seconds later her slippers scratched over the hardwood floors as she made her way to the kitchen. When she saw Nine and Gates in the same room she knew there would be trouble.

"Take her out of here," Kerrick said slowly while glaring at her. He wanted her to know this was her fault too. "And get her cleaned up."

"Sure, honey," she said weakly walking to her grandchild. "I'm so sorry, husband. Please forgive me."

It was clear that everyone feared him, even his own wife.

When they were gone Kerrick faced Gates. "That was my granddaughter." He shuffled around uneasily as he considered if he should kill him again. He'd seen too much. "She's mentally ill."

"I understand," he lied before clearing his throat. "Did she have whips on her back? Or was I seeing things?"

"Of course not," he responded as if he were highly offended. "Do I look like I would do something so horrible? To my own grandchild at that?"

Gates had been in the game long enough to know that he had to be careful in that moment. Kerrick was a certified killer. And whatever went on in his home was Kerrick's problem not his. So he cleared his throat and grabbed the wine that was on the counter. "Got glasses?"

A bright light shined on Nine, which presented her body as if she were art at an exhibit. Butterscotch colored leather cuffs bound her wrists. They were connected to chains, which extended from the ceiling. On her ankles black leather cuffs held her in place forcing her limbs to be stretched outward. Her big toes were the only things touching the floor of the basement.

When Nine was strapped securely, Kerrick removed his blue suit jacket and tossed it on a black chair in the middle of the floor. He unbuttoned his white-cuffed shirt and rolled his sleeves up to his elbow. Then he grabbed the black leather whip sitting in the corner.

Sweat poured down Nine's face and her body shivered. She had her menstruation cycle so tiny splatters of blood sprayed on the floor below her. She was used to this part of her life. The part where he beat her for one reason or another. During these times she would mentally escape to one of the places she read about in the many books in her collection. Usually she went to Rome, or China where she could become a different person, under a different circumstance. No matter where she escaped mentally, the pain was always real.

Before Kerrick beat her he examined the structure of her body. She was shaped like a goddess and parts of his soul felt guilty for looking at her in a sexual way. Still, his desires could not be controlled.

Nine invaded his soul. It took him years to understand why he hated her so much. Until one day she was staring down at him and he saw her eyes. She looked…just…like…Thandi. His wife in Africa who was murdered for his sins. Her dark skin. Her perfect features. Her soft sexuality that seemed to exacerbate the older she got. He was never turned on by any of his offspring but when it came to Nine he was enamored.

Instead of giving in to his desires he beat her. Abused her. Demeaned her. Hoping that if he whipped the flesh off of her bones that she would be less appealing. Instead she grew stronger and her sexual appeal shined brighter with each torture section he orchestrated.

Nine's life was hard. She lived in a dark room in the basement, a few doors over from the torture room. She didn't have any furniture outside of a twin bed, a desk, one chair and a lamp. She only had two outfits in her possession. A long white muumuu that drowned out her shape, but never hiding her beautiful face. She also owned a black muumuu that she had outgrown due to her growing curves.

Kerrick ran his hand down the leather whip and slapped it against the floor, sending a thwack sound throughout the basement. He did it again to strike fear in her heart. It worked. Nine's face squinted as if she'd already been struck.

"I had a meeting today and you embarrassed me," he said speaking of Gates.

Thwack.

He struck her on the back and her body trembled like the strings on a guitar.

"I'm sorry, grandfather," she apologized as she struggled to endure the pain. "I didn't mean to interrupt but I was hungry."

Thwack.

He struck her again and she tensed up, forcing her buttocks to tighten before they relaxed.

"Do you realize the amount of money I might have lost with your antics?" He paused. "Do you?" He yelled.

"It's all my fault, grandfather," she sobbed. "I should've waited for Fran. But I haven't seen her in days and I wanted something to eat."

Nine had learned a long time ago that going against Kerrick was futile. If she wanted to survive this lashing she would have to be agreeable, and endure everything he dished. He beat her twenty times, until her body went limp and her head fell forward before she passed out.

When he was done, Kerrick wiped the sweat off of his face with the back of his hand. He tossed the whip to the floor and walked slowly toward her. He ran the back of his hand over her face, the only place on her body he preserved. He wanted it to remain perfect and yet he didn't know why.

"You haunt me," he whispered even though she was unconscious. "You're going to be the death of me. I just know it. So why can't I kill you?"

CHAPTER TWELVE
NINE

"I do not ask much. I beg cold comfort."
-William Shakespeare

Nine lie on her stomach while Fran nursed her wounds with peroxide. She winced a little even though Fran's touch was delicate and careful. "He almost killed you," Fran said as tears rolled down her face. "I don't know what I would've done if he would've taken you from me." She paused and looked into Nine's eyes. "Like he took the baby from my body I never got the chance to love."

"This isn't your fault, Fran," Nine whispered, barely having enough energy to speak. I should've stayed in my room. The blame belongs to me."

Fran yanked Nine's chin and forced her closer. "No. Don't ever apologize for surviving." Her words were firm and serious. She released her and tended to her wounds again. "I got upset with your grandfather and I left you here alone for two days." She looked at her with sorrow. "But I will never leave you again."

Nine knew she was lying. The bottle was the only thing she was loyal to but it still felt good to hear.

Francesca, Kerrick's long time lover had reached the bottom of her life. When Kerrick turned her on to drugs many years ago, and killed any chance she had of having children by jabbing a knife into her womb she was determined to prove to him that she could get clean off drugs again. So she went into hiding, and then into rehab despite Kerrick's threats to haunt her down if she left town.

Within six months Fran was getting her life on track. She had relocated to Florida and even met new friends. But she could still recall the day he found her.

The sun shined brightly on her bronzing skin as she soaked up the rays. When all of a sudden she felt a dark presence. Her eyes widened when through her tinted shades she was staring at Kerrick.

He threw a plane ticket on her stomach; next to the wound he caused which made her barren. "You had better be on that flight in the morning. Or I will kill anybody who knows your name." He walked away and suddenly the bright beach seemed dark and evil.

Fran disobeyed him and Kerrick had proven to be a man of his word. When she got a new boyfriend Kerrick would have him killed. When she got a secret lover, Kerrick would have him tortured and murdered. She was his property and there was no escape.

Realizing he was serious she went back to Maryland where she stayed for six months. He would use her body as often as he liked and when he was done he'd give her money for her worries. Instead of spending it Fran decided to stack her cash and after awhile she saved $10,000 and took a flight to Honduras. She was there for a year, living in a little cottage she owned outside of a small village. Although it looked like she planned the ultimate escape she was wrong.

Kerrick found her and had some locals place her in a dark hole with no light. For an entire month he would have her beaten, starved and raped with foreign objects. They would prevent her from going to sleep, starve her and every night the men would make her say Kerrick's name until her tongue dried. When they were finished with her she begged to see his face. He was like an angel.

When she was released he told her the debt was not paid. He forced her to be his maid and cook and clean for his family. She left one prison and entered another. She never tried to escape again and avoided drugs at all costs. But her new poison was alcohol, which had proven to be a loyal companion.

As the days went by Fran couldn't decide which was the real hell. Her time in Honduras or seeing Victoria prance around the mansion with diamond rings and fur housecoats, knowing that she had the life that was rightfully hers. Although Fran knew about Victoria, Victoria was clueless about who Fran really was. And Kerrick threatened to crucify her if she so much as looked at his wife in the wrong way.

So Fran cooked meals for his family, cleaned the house and massaged Victoria's feet when she was tired after a long day of gardening or shopping. Sometimes she wished for death thinking that it may have been better. That is until he put her in charge of caring for baby Nine. Taking care of Kelly's last daughter gave her a reason to live.

Nine's mother checked out on life a long time ago after Kerrick disowned her. So Fran took care of her twelve-month old infant as if she were her own. And Nine loved her hard.

Kerrick assumed that Nine was a throwaway, nothing more than a person living in his home who ate when he felt like feeding her. He was unaware of how intelligent Fran was in her former life and what she was instilling in his 9th and last grandchild.

Prior to Kerrick entering Fran's life, she won a scholarship to John Hopkins University to study medicine but her passion was always literature. That was until she met up with Money Mouse and forgot all about an education. However, her love for books remained strong. She relished in the words of Shakespeare, Edgar Allen Poe and other great writers. And she made sure Nine appreciated the art of literature too.

Although Nine loved fiction novels she gravitated more toward books about serial killers. She became interested in what inspired a human being to take a life. And this never set right with Fran. She was worried she was just like her grandfather.

After Fran nursed her wounds she fed Nine chicken noodle soup and crackers. When she was fed she read

Shakespeare's *Romeo and Juliet* to her out loud. Fran was composed until she reached a certain point in the story.

> *"My bounty is as boundless as the sea,*
> *My love as deep; the more I give to thee,*
> *The more I have, for both are infinite."*

Nine didn't see Fran crying. Instead she was mesmerized as she always was whenever Fran read the story with so much passion. "I want a love like that," Nine said daydreaming.

Fran slammed the book shut, which startled Nine. "You don't want a love like that! You want to be smarter than love! Much smarter."

"I'm sorry," Nine whispered upon upsetting Fran. "I didn't mean to anger you."

"Don't be sorry, just listen to me. Your only concern should be figuring out what a person wants from you and then using that power against them. Love is not worth your life, Nine. Or your time. Always remember. Take it from me, I know."

"Why do you still love him?" Nine asked softly. "If he caused you so much pain." Nine was the only one in the home, besides Kerrick, who knew that Fran had a past relationship with her grandfather and she was always intrigued about why. In Nine's eyes he was pure evil.

"He fulfilled the weakness in me. And I allowed him."

When the bedroom door flew open Kelly walked inside with a jar of cream. "You are dismissed now," she said to Fran as if she was an afterthought. "It's time for her treatment."

Fran stood up, bowed and said, "Yes, mam. I'm leaving now."

Fran hated what Kelly had started doing to Nine. Although Kerrick held her to the agreement to leave him alone, she still hoped to gain his love by bleaching Nine's skin. "Nine, get out of the bed," she ordered.

"Mother, I'm in a lot of pain." Her body still ached from the abuse Kerrick caused her earlier. "Do we have—"

"You want your grandfather to love you right?" Kelly yelled interrupting her daughter.

"Yes, mother. More than anything."

"Then you have to do what I'm asking. Now get out of bed, stand up and face the wall."

Nine limped toward her and Kelly removed her nightgown. She placed her hands on the wall and prepared herself for more pain. Kelly smoothed the cream everywhere even over the fresh wounds Kerrick caused. She was a mental case who was confused and not tapped into what she was doing or who she was hurting. She lived in her mind. Which was a dangerous place.

"I know you think I don't love you but I do," Kelly said as she continued to press the cream into her chocolate skin. "If you knew how much I had to give up to keep you alive you'd understand why this is necessary."

Kelly's one-track mind when it came to her grandfather was the reason that her older sister Paige, who

Nine had never met, ran away from the house after her sister Lydia was killed. She never returned home and after awhile nobody continued to look for her. She was worthless. The saddest part is that neither Kelly nor Avery realized she was gone until five days later.

Nine continued to squint as the cream washed into her exposed flesh.

"In case you're wondering, I chose your life over the love from my father," she said as she did a million times before. "The least you could do is care about my feelings instead of your own. You only get one mother, Nine. And unfortunately I'm yours."

CHAPTER THIRTEEN
AUTUMN 'LEAF' LINCOLN

"Tempt not a desperate man."
-William Shakespeare

The scent from Autumn's new leather coat wafted above the teenagers' head as he sat in the gymnasium of Fredrick Douglas High School in Baltimore City. They were watching the basketball team lose another game against Eleanor Roosevelt. The shit was getting boring at best.

Four of Autumn's friends surrounded him, ready to give their lives with the wave of his hand. Besides, he was a Lincoln. In the drug world his last name carried as much weight as the Prophet Family but he never threw around his power.

Autumn, who went by the nickname Leaf because he felt his birth name was too soft, had an easygoing personality. He didn't boast about his family association. He believed in letting every man judge him on his actions and not how he could have their life snuffed out at any moment if he desired.

He was smart. He was fair and he was also generous. But he had one problem. He loved girls, especially those who were unavailable. There was something about a girl who never looked his way, which rarely happened, that made him want her even more.

Leaf rubbed his hand backwards through his curly mane. His khaki colored skin was flawless and the gold chain that hung around his neck was speckled with high-end diamonds, which shined clear across the auditorium. He was a king and he knew it.

When his friend's saw his attention diverted they decided to mess with his head. "Who's bitch you looking at this time?" Bops asked as he ate a bag of chips on the bleachers. Bops was a foster care kid who was loyal to a fault. He once smacked a teacher who told Leaf that his money wouldn't give him a pass in his class if he didn't show up. Leaf didn't necessarily agree with hitting a public official, but he liked his fire and allowed him in his crew because of it.

"I haven't found one yet," he replied as he scanned the room again. "It's the same chicks in this school. Maybe I should start finding my girls at colleges."

"You can't find nothing here because you already ran through everything in the building," Mole responded.

Mole was a huge kid with large freckles who migrated from Washington DC when his mother got a job managing a McDonald's on Rolling Road. He begged a lot but because Leaf knew he would kill for him, he didn't mind looking out from time-to-time, as long as he didn't go too far. Besides, Leaf had more money than he could spend. His father Justin and mother Corrine Lincoln, were real estate moguls in the city. It was whispered that the real estate company was nothing more than a drug front for a Cartel out of Mexico. But it couldn't be proven and those who kept talking about it found themselves breathing in dirt.

"I'm getting tired of easy conquests," Leaf said as he continued his stationary hunt. "I want a challenge."

"Did this nigga just say conquest?" Bops joked slapping Mole on the arm.

"Don't get mad at me because your vocabulary is limited. You gotta have word play if you want to bag these bitches these days. They be reading them books and shit."

Leaf knew about a proper word game although he rarely used it. He had a 4.0 grade point average, which was another reason he was interesting. He barely came to school but when he did he excelled. The school board wanted to throw him out but since his work was exemplary when he showed up, they couldn't justify an expulsion. Leaf could've transferred to a private school but he wouldn't hear of it. Public schools had real people and bad bitches so he told his parents he would stay where he was. And as an only child he always got what he wanted.

"Fuck that shit," Bops said. "All you need is a big dick and some paper and you can have any girl you want. They don't care 'bout no word game."

"He's right but I know somebody you haven't bagged yet," Mole said.

"Who?" Leaf asked curiously.

"Chloe."

Leaf tuned him out just as Chloe walked in with Keaton. Mole was right. To the day, Chloe had remained untouched by him. Her blue jeans looked painted on as she switched through the auditorium toward the bleachers. Every step she took caused her ass to jiggle. Her hazelnut colored complexion gave her a baked appeal and Leaf's dick stiffened when she ran her pink tongue over her lips. He wanted her. But there was one problem, her nigga, Keaton.

Keaton's father ran some projects in Baltimore city but Leaf's family owned the buildings, this fact is what determined the Lincoln Estates were nothing more than a drug front.

Ordinarily Leaf would respect Keaton and leave his bitch alone but Chloe was just too sexy to ignore. It wasn't like he didn't try getting at her though. He would brush past her in the hallway intentionally and she wouldn't even bat an eye his way. He would throw elaborate parties at the extra house his family owned in a Baltimore suburb, invite her and Keaton, and he would show up without her. He did all he could to get her attention and nothing worked. Oh yes. He wanted her badly. She was a challenge.

As the basketball game continued he stared her down as if he could see through her clothes. And when she whispered in Keaton's ear, grabbed her purse and walked down the bleachers, the entire gym paused as if they were about to sing the pledge of allegiance.

Although Leaf knew Keaton's background he knew nothing about Chloe's. She came to the high school last year and the next thing he knew she was on Keaton's arm. The travesty was that Leaf didn't even get a chance to lay down his pimp game first. He wasn't at school that day. It was the one day he regretted playing hooky because he missed his opportunity. But hindsight was twenty-twenty.

"Damn, that bitch bad," Mole said with his jaw hung as she walked toward the exit.

"I'll eat her pussy on her period," Bops said.

His friends were right. She was cold. Leaf decided that he was going to meet Chloe in front of the girl's bathroom. Since the boy's bathroom was on the other end, he hung around the water fountain as if he wanted a sip. He knew she went inside because he could smell her expensive perfume lingering in the air. Leaf knew quality when he smelled it because his mother only wore the best.

When she came out of the bathroom, Leaf bent down and took a sip from the fountain. Chloe stood behind him waiting. He wiped his mouth and allowed her a drink. She smiled and bent down to get a sip. Her back arched sending her ass straight up in the air. It looked as if the sun had risen and Leaf was gone.

"I was wondering when you were going to make your move," she said as she rose up and wiped her mouth with her fingertips. Her lips glistened. "You move too slowly, Lincoln." She turned around and allowed her eyes to roll over him as if he were a brand new luxury car.

"I don't know what you talking about," he lied while trying to remain cool.

She giggled. "Lincoln, let's keep it real. You be brushing up against me in the hallway, sending me invites to your little parties and shit. All I'm saying is that everything you doing ain't hard enough for me. If you want this pussy, you gotta come stronger."

Leaf was shocked. In all of his life he never met a chick with game more thorough than his. The way she ignored him at school he didn't think she knew he existed. He would have to play it cool or Chloe could have his mind fucked up.

He decided to call her bluff. "I'm trying to fuck. That hard enough?"

She pushed off of the wall, grabbed the collar of his shirt and pulled him with her into the girl's bathroom like a dog. She pushed open the green stall door and they both strutted inside as if they were one.

She sat her Louis Vuitton purse on the piss soaked floor and Leaf watched as she pushed her jeans and red panties to her ankles. The curves of her body were as sexy as he envisioned. She turned around and placed her hands on the graffiti covered bathroom stall as if she were under arrest. The diamond rings on her fingers sparkled along with the $5,000 tennis bracelet on her wrist.

As he eyed her body he couldn't believe his luck. The anticipation and chase had been so extensive that he never imagined it would go down like this. He felt like he was on cloud nine until he remembered he was a Lincoln. He was a king. And shit like this should happen to him all the time.

So he removed his dick from his jeans and pushed into her pussy. It was warm as her walls squeezed his shaft. He placed his hands on her waist and slow fucked her before going hard. Her moans were not too loud. Not too strong. But heavily erotic. Her tongue eased out of her mouth and she licked her lips as if she just ate a spoonful of her favorite ice cream.

Leaf pushed in and dipped out of her soggy box until he exploded inside of her as if she belonged to him. No doubt it was everything he wanted it to be.

Chloe eased her clothes up and he zipped his jeans.

She turned around and looked into his eyes. She winked and kissed him softly. "I knew we would fuck good together." Her face was prettier up close.

"Then we have to do it again," he admitted.

"Anytime." She kissed him gently, leaving a peppermint trail on his lips before she walked out the bathroom.

CHAPTER FOURTEEN
NINE

"Is there no pity sitting in the clouds, that sees into the bottom of my grief?"
-William Shakespeare

Nine was lying in bed staring up at the dark ceiling. Her mind was flooded with hopes, desires and aspirations for her life. Even though she never had one. In the books she read over and over she learned of worlds outside of the mansion but how could she access them? She was confined like a dark ugly secret. Her grandfather hated her. Her mother cared more about how Nine looked than how she felt and her father only gave her charity smiles.

Feeling frustrated she rolled over on her side and cried. She needed an escape and if one didn't come soon she was afraid she would act aggressively.

Lately Nine had evil thoughts and a sensation to express herself violently. She could no longer count the times she became aroused while envisioning stabbing or killing another human being. Isolation and limited contact with people was causing her to see them as objects, and she didn't want that. She wanted to love. She wanted to dream. She wanted to live.

The remorse for her evil feelings was so great that she prayed to the God Fran told her existed. The one who answered everyone's prayers but hers. But nothing worked. She had developed an appetite for inflicting pain on others and she would soon see it realized.

She rolled over onto her other side and tried to go to sleep but the hunger pangs in her gut was making it difficult. She hadn't eaten a bite since yesterday morning and her stomach groaned until she heard laughter in the larger part of the house. Curious, she eased off of the bed and tiptoed toward the door. She pressed her ear against it and listened attentively. When she heard *her* voice she trembled.

Horrified, Nine backed away from the door and sat on the chair at her desk. Five minutes later twenty-one year old Alice, Kerrick's prized granddaughter, entered. Her eyes were as evil as her spirit but no one would know it. Besides the monster was beautiful. Her light brown hair had long cascading curls and her cheeks were naturally blushed. Her eyes were hazel and her lips were rose colored giving her an innocent appeal when she was anything but. The black dress she wore hugged her curves and she brought an air of doom with her.

Alice was a sick young woman who had been molested by her father all of her life. And now she was acting out on others.

Alice strutted deeper into the room holding a brown paper bag in her hand. She wasn't supposed to be in Nine's room. As far as Kerrick knew no one but those who lived in the mansion knew she existed. But Alice, on a hunt to feed the weed habit she developed one day found her two years ago. When she asked Kerrick if anyone else lived there but them, he said of course not.

That was Alice's queue to do with Nine what she willed. And she did a lot.

Alice closed the door behind her and leaned against it. "Hello, number Nine. How are you?"

Nine sat in her seat trembling. She feared Alice more than anything. Kerrick, although brutal, activated restraint when he abused her. There were things he wouldn't do like touch her face or take her life. With Alice Nine couldn't be sure. She got the impression that if she did or said the wrong thing Alice would have her murdered and she was right.

"I brought food," Alice said raising the greasy bag in the air. "Hungry.

Nine's bladder released and urine soaked her left foot before splashing against the floor. Alice scared her that much.

"Oh my goodness, you've wet yourself again," Alice said in a condescending tone. The more Nine was afraid, the wetter Alice's pussy grew. "Aren't you happy I came to visit you? Outside of that dirty maid I know you don't have any friends. But thank God you can always count on me."

Nine nodded her head slowly although it was a lie.

Alice removed a piece of fried chicken from the bag. She strolled closer to Nine and placed it under her nose. "Doesn't it smell good?"

Nine's mouth began to salivate and she licked her lips. "Yes," she responded, her upper lip brushing against the seasoned crust.

"Lick it," Alice ordered.

Nine was about to bite it instead but Alice said, "If you bite it, bitch I will kill you."

Nine swallowed the air in her throat and licked the chicken. She tasted the saltiness and her stomach grumbled. "That's a nice little slave," she cheered. "She walked over to the bed, removed her black heels and said, "Now come lick my foot. And I'll give you a bite of my drumstick."

Nine was about to rush toward her when she said, "You know the rules, number nine." She pointed to the floor. "Always approach me on your knees."

Nine dropped to the floor and crawled toward her. A trail of urine followed as she moved. When Nine made it to Alice, she placed the bottom of her foot in her face. Nine ran her tongue up and down the heel of her foot before licking her toes. When she was done Alice's foot was clean.

Alice's box juiced up and she hated herself for being so aroused by Nine. There was something extremely seductive about her. Something regal. In a way, although she was confined to a room, Nine was God like. Which is why she took pleasure in dominating her.

Horny, Alice placed the bag on the bed, raised her dress and played with her pussy until she exploded on her fingertips. When she was done she kicked Nine in the face and said, "Keep your fucking hands off of me! Before I tell grandfather on you! You know how much he loves me." She grabbed the chicken and stomped toward the door.

Nine wrestled with whether to say something to her about the deal they just made. A year ago she wouldn't dare speak to her unless Alice asked a question. But with each day Nine was changing.

So she licked her lips, and swallowed the taste of Alice's dirty feet from her mouth. "Cousin," she said softly. "May I have the chicken like you promised?"

"No you may not, bitch. Now that you licked it I have to throw it in the trash anyway. I don't want nothing you ate in my body." She rushed out and slammed the door behind her.

CHAPTER FIFTEEN
NINE

"O Romeo, Romeo! Wherefore art thou Romeo?"
-William Shakespeare

Nine was sitting at her desk reading her books. The lamp above the pages illuminated the novel that held her attention, taking her mind off her hunger for the moment. It was ten o'clock at night and she was reading *The Life And Times Of Ted Bundy: The World's Most Charismatic Serial Killer.*

If she wasn't reading Shakespeare's works, she was studying serial killers. She wasn't interested in the ones who were caught early on after only murdering a person or two. She was only engaged if they killed twenty or more.

She ran her finger over the cool page and read it out loud:

"Ted Bundy was described as both charismatic and friendly, but behind the facade was the twisted mind of a serial killer. In just four years, he was able to kidnap and kill 30 young women in the United States. Sometimes he would pretend to be an authority figure or a disabled person to lure his victims. But on other instances he would approach them with a smile, win them over, rape them and dismember their bodies. He often kept their heads as souvenirs."

"Nine! Nine! Don't you hear me talking to you?" Nine heard a voice call from behind.

She slammed the book shut, turned around and saw her grandfather standing in front of her. His face was crinkled in anger. He placed a plate on her desk as he stood over top of her. A half eaten steak, a few mashed potatoes and green beans sat on top of it. She wanted to dive in but his expression froze her movements.

"I'm sorry, grandfather. I was reading."

Kerrick lifted the heavy book and read the title. "Why would you be reading something so violent?" he asked as if he hadn't beat her with whips, murdered people for sport and kept her locked in a room in the basement. "Putting this sort of filth into your mind is not good."

"I don't know, grandfather. It brings me pleasure."

He gave her an accusatory glare and dropped the heavy book on the table. The desk rocked slightly. "Where is Fran?"

"I don't know."

His gazed bounced around her room. "When you see her tell her I—"

"Kerrick, come right away," Victoria yelled as she appeared in the doorway. "Something terrible has happened."

Hearing the fear in his wife's voice, Kerrick rushed toward the door. Before he exited Nine said, "Grandfather, I'm sorry I disrespected your dinner party the other week, and forced you to have to beat me. I only pray that I can work to earn your forgiveness."

Kerrick was surprised that she spoke to him. In a way he was proud but he would never show it. Instead he scanned over her and walked out to tend to his wife. As always he closed and locked the door behind him.

Nine scoffed down the food and waited five minutes before curiosity got the best of her. What had her grandmother so shook? When she couldn't take it anymore she crept toward her bed, raised the mattress and grabbed a six-inch metal rod. She rushed toward the door, inserted the object in the keyhole and it popped open. She was a master at opening locked doors, a secret she didn't even share with Fran.

When it was open she exited the room and entered another door off of the basement. Inside was a huge generator along with the heating and air-conditioning systems used to operate the estate. Behind the walls of the mansion, Nine walked up the man made staircase that led to an air duct and crawled in until she reached the vent that connected to the living room.

Through the slits she saw a handsome older light skin man, a beautiful white woman and a teenager with curly hair who was covered in blood. Her heart skipped several beats when she saw the teenager's face. He was very attractive and she wondered why she'd never seen him before.

When she heard their voices Nine focused on the conversation.

"Kerrick, I realize I haven't seen you in years, but I need your help," the man said.

Kerrick gazed over the teenager and then the white woman. "Corrine, can you leave us alone please?"

"Sure," she said with a quivering voice. Something clearly upset her.

Kerrick waited until she disappeared before speaking to the man. "After everything you've done, Justin. Give me one reason why I should protect you."

When Nine accidently bumped the inside of the vent the conversation ceased. He turned toward the sound and walked over to the vent to check it out. He realized it was nothing.

CHAPTER SIXTEEN
LEAF
EARLIER THAT DAY

"The strength of twenty men."
-William Shakespeare

The cafeteria was bustling with the sounds of teenagers eating and chatting about their lives and troubles. Leaf on the other hand, didn't have a care in the world. He was at the table with Chloe, the baddest bitch in the high school. The other teenagers whispered about them and everybody wondered what would happen now that Leaf Lincoln had snagged the unattainable Chloe, who still had a man.

When Bops saw everyone was focused on his friend instead of their cold pizza he leaned over to Leaf and said, "I don't like this shit, man. The nigga seemed real mad in math class. He don't like how ya'll been going hard over the past few days."

To the right of Leaf was Chloe and to her right were her friends who all thought she should've been with Leaf a long time ago. In their minds, there was nothing better than a Lincoln but another Lincoln.

"I'm with, Bops," Mole said as he sucked down a bite of pizza. "The nigga been eyeing you crazy. I think we gonna have to roll on him."

Although his friends were worried Leaf was unbothered. He leaned toward them so that Chloe couldn't hear his words. He doubted she would anyway since her and her friends had been running their mouths non-stop about how cute Leaf was.

"So I'm supposed to be mad that he can't control his bitch?"

"This nigga's a hothead, Leaf," Bops said seriously. "You already fucked her. Maybe you should scale back on the quality time and shit. That's all I'm saying."

"Who said I fucked her?" he smiled.

Although he loved the ladies he never told his friends details. They always formed their opinions based on how the girls acted when he cut them off. Chloe was the first girl he ever spent time with after he hit. He had to admit, she was interesting.

"It don't matter if you did or didn't," Mole said. "Keaton think you did and he out for blood."

Leaf brushed his friends off. Besides, he had never been afraid of anybody or anything and he wasn't about to start now.

Leaf placed his arm around Chloe's neck and whispered in her ear just as Keaton came through the cafeteria's door. Everyone else paused anticipating his next move.

Keaton scanned the lunchroom until he found who he was looking for…Chloe.

"I put something in your coat pocket," Bops whispered to his friend. "Use it if you have to."

Leaf didn't know what it was but he wasn't interested in using it anyway. Keaton was a punk with a broken heart and he saw no reason to have to get into gangster shit with him.

Keaton stomped over toward Chloe and said, "Get your shit and let's go," he grabbed her forearm and tried to pull her up but she wouldn't move. "You've gone too far now. Let's go talk."

"Keaton, get your hands off her," Leaf said, minus the aggression.

Instead of respecting that Leaf did not punch him in the jaw, his coolness angered Keaton even more. Keaton's life was crumbling around him and yet Leaf performed as if he didn't have a care in the world.

"I don't have a problem with you conversing with her but you have to ask her nicely," Leaf responded. "And if she says yes she's free to go with you. I'm not holding her hostage."

Frustrated, Keaton created a fist and moved to punch Leaf when everyone at the table stood up in his defense. Leaf remained seated, with a smile planted on his face. Seeing that he was outnumbered Keaton backed up. "Who the fuck you think you are, Leaf?" he asked with tears streaming down his face although he wasn't sobbing. "You think you can just take a nigga's bitch and that's it?"

"First off I didn't take your bitch. Like I said all you gotta do is ask her to leave," Leaf said. "What you waiting on?"

Keaton looked down at Chloe's beautiful face. He wanted to ask but there was one thing stopping him. What would happen if she said no? So he took a deep breath. "Chloe, I love you," he said softly. "And we made plans to spend our lives together. There ain't nothing this nigga can buy you that I can't," he said pointing at Leaf. "All I'm asking is that you give me another chance."

Chloe was so embarrassed at his softness that her face reddened. She looked back at Leaf and Leaf said, "Don't be rude, mami. He's talking to you."

She focused back on Keaton.

"If you want to break up with me that's cool, but don't do it like this," Keaton continued. "Please. Come with me and let's talk."

Chloe was as cold as an Alaskan glacier. "I'm sorry, Keaton. But I'm chilling right now."

Keaton's face contorted from sadness into rage. His teeth showed and spit hung around the corners of his mouth. He looked like a rabid dog and he was about to pull Chloe apart before Leaf stopped him…verbally.

"If you touch her you gonna be paralyzed," he said smoothly. He didn't even give him the courtesy of looking his way. Instead he busied himself with the pizza on his plate. "You do enjoy walking," he took a bite of his pizza, "right?" This time he looked directly into Keaton's eyes so that he'd know he was real.

There it was. The killer that Keaton knew existed but never saw. "I'm leaving now," Keaton said eyeing the army that stood behind Leaf. "But I want you to know this, Chloe. His family fucks each other and has kids. You better not get pregnant by this dude. Unless you want a retard for a child." He rushed out before Leaf ordered the attack.

Everybody who stood in Leaf's honor took a seat. "Fuck that nigga talking 'bout?" Bops asked. "Ole' jealous ass nigga mad cause his bitch hanging on Leaf's dick."

"I don't even know, cuz," Leaf responded.

He tried to pretend as if Keaton's words didn't bring him confusion. What about his family did Keaton know that he wasn't privy to? When he realized Keaton was just hating he brushed it off. If this was a prizefight it would be a knock out and he decided to leave it at that.

Later on that day when class was over Leaf strutted to his locker. When he opened the door a letter smelling of sweet perfume dropped out. He smiled and looked around for Chloe. He hoped it was another picture of her pussy because she loved to take them and he loved to look at them. But when he picked it up and read it there was only a letter inside.

Dear Leaf,

I'm so sorry about what Keaton did today in the cafeteria. He doesn't understand that you and I have something beautiful. Something I'm not willing to give up. So I broke up with him. I told him I love you. I'm ready to spend my life with you if you'll have me.

I'll meet you by your truck later. I can't wait to see you.

Love your girlfriend,
Chloe

Leaf felt gut punched as he refolded the letter and stuffed it in his locker. Why she had to go so deep? Damn! He wasn't trying to be in a relationship. He was just fucking her and the fact that she had a nigga who wanted her was part of the appeal. Truth be told with Keaton out of the picture she wasn't as interesting anymore.

Leaf grabbed his jacket, left everything else in his locker and walked toward his black Escalade parked at the curb. At first he was going to leave without saying bye but Chloe had the sweetest sex he ever had. He owed her an explanation.

Five minutes later Chloe came outside. But Leaf also saw Keaton standing on the top of the steps looking at him. He stood out because teenagers zipped around him as if he were a fixture on the building and yet his gaze remained on Leaf. The feeling Leaf felt when he saw the look on his face was the closest he ever came to being afraid. Now he wished he hadn't sent Bops and Mole on their way.

His attention was broken momentarily when Chloe rushed toward him wearing a wide smile on her face. "Hey, baby," she grinned kissing him on the cheek. "I've been waiting to see you all day. Did you get the letter I left in your locker?"

Leaf looked at Keaton while he spoke to her. He wanted to keep eyes on him in case he made a move. "Yea, but I can't see you no more. I'm sorry."

She backed up from him and held her belly. "What…what are you talking about?"

When he saw the flushed look on her face he felt bad but he had to keep it real. "You cool and everything but I'm not feeling you like you feeling me."

"Is it because you're scared of him? Because I can have my father take him out."

Leaf took offense and frowned. "I'm not even scared of God."

Her lips trembled. "Then what did I do?" she yelled causing students walking by to look at them. "I fucked you and now you trying to carry me like some stank bitch?"

"I'm sorry you feel that way but—"

His sentence was cut off when he saw the gun in her hand. Where did she get it? It didn't matter because her finger slid on the trigger. He tried to defend himself by knocking her to the ground with a blow to her cheek. The gun flew out of her hand and clanked against the ground, letting off one shot in the air.

With wide eyes seeing the melee, Keaton rushed toward them.

And that's when Leaf remembered. Bops had placed something in his jacket pocket during lunchtime. He stuffed his hand in his leather jacket and pulled out a pocketknife. He hit the button on the handle and it flew open just as Chloe grabbed the gun and prepared to shoot him in the penis.

Leaf slashed her face with the knife and when she maintained possession of the gun he slit her throat. Blood splattered all over his shoes, clothes and truck. And when he looked up he saw everyone holding their mouths in horror. There he was standing by his Escalade with a knife in his hand. He just committed murder.

Keaton, who made it down the stairs, dropped to his knees and picked up Chloe's bleeding body.

Leaf jumped into his truck and rushed away from the scene.

After Kerrick heard the entire story he slammed down on the sofa in the living room. Not only had killing Chloe caused a problem in Justin's life, it caused a problem for him too.

"You're going to have to stay here until I figure things out," Kerrick said to his son. "Both of you." He looked at Leaf. "I'm sure once the media gets a hold of this it will be crazy."

"Can somebody tell me what's going on?" Leaf asked, having no idea that the man who's home he was in was his grandfather.

"Leaf, just go to the den with your mother. I'll explain things when I can."

"Dad—"

"Just go," he yelled.

Defeated, Leaf followed orders.

"When are you going to tell him that he is my grandson? And that he is a Prophet and not a Lincoln?"

"Never," Justin professed. "I don't like what's going on in this house. How you encouraged my sisters and brothers to nest. And I will not subject my only son to this family's secrets." He paused. "Now if you don't want to help me I understand. We'll just leave and you won't hear from me for another five years."

Kerrick's age was causing his heart to soften when it came to his family. In the past he was able to control them. But that was then. His children were adults now. The last thing he wanted was something happening to his favorite kids. "The boy must stay here where my men can protect him. And if you want me to deny who he is to me I will."

Relieved Justin said, "Thank you, father." It was the first time he called him father in years.

CHAPTER SEVENTEEN
NINE

"You tread upon my patience."
-William Shakespeare

Nine was standing next to her desk looking at Alice and the strange man she brought with her. As always when she saw her cousin her body convulsed and she felt as if she were about to explode.

Alice's face was painted as beautifully as ever and her hair was combed back into a neat ponytail. The navy blue cardigan sweater she wore made her look more like a teacher than a predator.

"Nine, this is my friend Hector." She locked the door and stepped toward her holding his hand. "He wanted to say hello." Alice squeezed his hand and said, "Say hello, Hector. Stop being weird."

"Hello," he said with lust in his eyes as he observed her.

He looked to be about her same age and his eyebrows were as curly as the nest sitting on top of his head. Although he was attractive he wasn't neatly trimmed and tamed. He looked as unraveled as his disposition.

"Come closer, Nine," Alice smiled. "Don't be afraid."

Slowly Nine walked toward her until she was as close as she could be. She breathed the expensive perfume that Alice wore that always made her sick. She hoped whatever she was about to do wouldn't be as bad as the last time, especially since Leaf and his parents were in the house.

"Turn around, Nine."

Nine turned around as slowly as the minute hand on a clock. She wasn't certain what was about to go down until a white cloth was draped over her head and forced into the center of her mouth. It was so tight it limited circulation to her lips.

Hector pushed her toward the table and said, "Hands on the desk, Nine." Hector certainly got comfortable quick.

Nine placed her hands on the desk and he raised her nightgown and it draped over her hips. She could hear Hector licking his lips in the background as he eyed her thick rear.

Alice gripped a fair amount of her ass and said, "See, she has good skin. Touch it, baby."

Hector ran his hands over Nine's ass before spreading her legs apart. When he couldn't take it anymore he came down on her ass with a metal object. It was a fireplace poker. Where had it come from? The pain was unbearable but Nine didn't cry. Instead she winced and her breath felt caught in her chest. Her life was a nightmare.

"Can I make love to her?" Hector begged Alice. "If you let me I will be quick."

Nine was frozen in fear because although she had been beaten, her virginity had remained in tact.

There was a long moment of silence before Alice slapped Hector so hard in the face he stumbled backwards. "You see how greedy you are?" she yelled. "I give you this pleasure and still you want more. Why can't this be enough? She's dirty anyway. I doubt if she takes more than one bath a week. And you talking about having sex?"

She was right. Once a week Kerrick allowed her to be bathed outside in the back of the house. If the weather was too cold she would have to wait until it would break.

Suddenly they grew silent. Although Nine could hear soft moans she couldn't see what was going on. How she wished they would leave her room. But she was powerless and knew she had no control.

When their sounds appeared muffled she slowly turned her head to the right. Now she could see Alice's dress raised over her head, covering her face, while Hector was on top of her making love. His dick may have been in her body but his eyes were on Nine's ass.

They spent an hour having sex while using her as an object in their sick expression. She decided that no matter what she had to get away from Alice and her games. Even if she had to die to protect herself, she was not going to take it anymore.

CHAPTER EIGHTEEN
NINE

"Past hope. Past cure. Past help."
-William Shakespeare

Nine had a nightmare that shook her out of her sleep. She was hanging in the basement of the mansion, handcuffed to the ceiling and the floor. Nobody had come to beat her, talk to her or feed her. Eventually she died from hunger, thirst and excruciating pain. She was drenched in sweat when she woke up and she rocked herself softly to calm down.

She was about to dose off again when she felt a presence in the room. Nine's eyes flew open and she saw Fran sitting on the edge of the bed smoking a cigarette. Nine wiped her wet forehead and said, "I can't count on you anymore, Fran. To feed me. And to make sure I'm okay. That wasn't always the case and it hurts my feelings. Why has that changed?"

Fran placed her cold hand on Nine's warm thigh. Her breath reeked of alcohol and cigarettes. The light blue uniform she wore was stained with dirt and her graying hair was disheveled. "I'm sorry," Fran said. "When I leave the mansion I often forget I'm alive. Until I remember you."

Nine eased out of bed and slowly walked to her desk. "I'm tired of apologies. They're useless." She sighed as she flipped open the cover to one of her books.

Fran's eyes widened because Nine had never spoken to her like that. Although shocked she was also proud. The fact that she was growing up and speaking out despite her conditions was the first mark of freedom. Fran saw strength brewing at the surface. Nine was almost ready to make an escape.

Fran eased off of the bed and stood in front of Nine. She looked into her eyes as if she were about to challenge her and Nine didn't flinch. Fran reached into her pocket and pulled out a .9 mm handgun. Nine stumbled into the desk, afraid of what Fran was about to do.

Fran's eyes appeared wild. She placed the barrel of the gun in Nine's face, put her finger on the trigger and pulled.

Nine's eyes closed, assuming her life was over. She was okay with it anyway because the current life left her loveless, hopeless and hungry. But when she realized she was not dead she opened her eyelids only to see the gun hanging at Fran's side.

"This is a nine millimeter handgun," Fran said as she handed the weapon to Nine. "Never be afraid of it again."

"But…but I thought you were about to shoot me." Nine said holding the heavy piece of artillery.

"Never be afraid of death either. It's life that causes you struggles." She paused. "Now come with me. I'm going to show you how to use it."

For the next few days Fran, an expert marksman, showed Nine how to load, unload, clean and operate the weapon. Although Fran never used the skill personally, she acquired it after years of running from Kerrick.

Still, Fran wanted Nine to always be able to protect herself. She could see her intelligence growing at a steady rate by the way she spoke up.

A few days later it was time for another one of Nine's lessons. She and Fran were out back, on the acres of land behind the mansion. The only other times Nine had been outside was to be bathed on a slab of concrete so she was always so mesmerized by the feel of the damp grass under her bare feet. They were far away from the property, where gunfire could not be heard at the house.

On any other day of training Nine was always focused. Today was different. Lately Leaf had been walking around the house and she found herself crawling through the ducts just to get a look at him. She was drawn to him in a way she couldn't explain and she didn't know why. The saddest part of it all was that he didn't know she existed. She was the girl in the walls. And unless he went snooping in the basement she doubted he ever would know her.

When she fired on the left of the target that was stuck on the tree instead of the middle, Fran snatched the gun out of her hand. "You've hit the target better than that in the past. Where is your mind, Nine? Tell me now."

She exhaled. "I…I was thinking—"

"Whenever you hold a gun, the only thing on your mind should be your target and your aim," she said interrupting her. "If your mind is on anything else it could cause you your life. Am I clear?"

Nine nodded.

"Good," Fran sighed.

Nine observed Fran. "Can I ask you a question?"

"Just ask."

"Are you teaching me how to shoot so that I can do what you never did? Kill grandfather?"

Fran's heart rate increased. Had this been her plan all along and she never knew it. "I'm giving you these skills because I love you. I'm giving you these skills because I want you to protect yourself. Whether your grandfather lives or dies is not in my thought process." She exhaled. "Anyway we're done with weapons training today. Let's work on your mental skills again. What's the first rule of seduction?" Fran asked in military fashion.

"When you're seducing, what you want doesn't matter."

"Correct," Fran said tucking the gun in the pocket of her uniform before dipping in the other to pull out a bottle of whiskey. She sat on the ground and Nine did also. Today was warmer than it had been over the past few days so it was relaxing. "I should've known the rules too." She twisted the top off and took a gulp. "Instead I allowed Kerrick to run my life so long that I didn't know what I wanted. Or what I needed."

"Is that why you don't want me to fall in love?"

"I don't want you to hurt, Nine. I'm going to give you all of the information I have. Tell you all of my mistakes so you can be smarter and learn from them." She took another gulp. "Otherwise what I've gone through was for nothing. Always learn the rules of seduction and perform as the Predator. Never the prey." She paused. "Let's go before someone realizes you're missing."

Fran snuck Nine back into her room. And when they opened the door, Leaf was standing by her desk holding one of her books.

CHAPTER NINETEEN
LEAF

"Rebellion lay in his way, and he found it."
-William Shakespeare

Leaf looked at the Latino maid and the girl standing in the doorway. He had been there for almost a week and he'd never seen Nine before.

"Hello." Fran said to him. "It's Autumn right?"

He put the book on the desk and said, "Yes. But I go by Leaf."

"I'm sorry for the mix up," she said wiping her sweaty palms on her uniform. "Uh…well Leaf, are you hungry?" she smiled. "I can go make you some food if you come with me upstairs."

She was doing her best to lure him away from Nine. Mainly because nobody outside of those who lived in the house knew she stayed there. Fran felt there was secrecy surrounding whom Leaf was. Prior to recently she'd never seen Justin and Corrine before. And when she asked Kerrick whom he and his family were he told her to stay out of his fucking business. His instructions for Fran were simple. Treat Leaf like a Prophet and that's all she needed to know.

Since Kerrick remained tight-lipped Fran drew her own opinions. Like everyone else who felt the members of the Prophet family looked the same, she suspected that Justin was upset about the inbreeding and disowned his family. Not even Nine knew that many members of her family were products of being brothers and sisters, including her parents. When Avery called Kerrick father Nine assumed because he was his father in law.

"I'm cool," he said politely, "but you can bring her something to eat if you want," he said pointing to Nine.

It was evident that he was not following Fran out of the room. "Well this is Nine," she said putting her hand on her shoulder. "She doesn't talk much but she's nice." After making her statement she walked out. She hoped he wouldn't stay long but more importantly, that he wouldn't mention to Kerrick that Nine had been out of her room.

"Is your name really Nine?" Leaf asked when they were alone.

Nine remained silent. She was told not to speak to outsiders if someone ever saw her. Although if there was one person she wanted to befriend he was it.

"So you really don't talk?" he continued, finding her intriguing. "I'm getting silence of the Nine?

She didn't laugh.

Although she wore a nightgown, her body was developing and Leaf noticed. Her hair was soft, wild and curly. Some might think it was untamed but he thought it gave her a unique appeal.

Her eyes were wide and although she looked frightened, there was something attractive about her he couldn't deny. He wanted to get to know the scraggly looking girl but who was she? She wasn't family, he was sure of that. Her complexion was rich chocolate and not vanilla colored like the others who lived there.

"Since you won't talk I'll call you Silent Nine."

Nine didn't say a word.

"Okay, that didn't go over either. You a tough crowd."

His eyes scanned the room and suddenly his nose caught up with it. It smelled faintly of urine and the air was as stale as old bread. There wasn't a window in sight and without the benefit of the lamp it would be pitch black. He looked at the old twin bed and then her desk. Was she being held hostage? "Do you live down here?"

Silence.

He walked up to her. "Why won't you talk to me?"

She walked around him and sat on the bed. At first she looked into his eyes and awaited his next question but due to how her stomach fluttered when she looked at him she quickly turned away. His presence freshened her room and she felt aroused.

"I get it," he smiled. "You want me gone. So just answer me this one question and I'll leave."

She focused on him. Now he held her attention. "Are you a Prophet?"

She swallowed and slowly shook her head no. She was right. Her mother told her over and over that her name was Nine. Nothing more. Nothing less.

He smiled as if relieved. "Okay."

He turned to walk out until she parted her lips. Because she had been silent for most of the day she licked her lips because they felt dry. "Please don't tell anyone you've been here."

He stopped and spun around until he was looking at the beautiful girl again. Her voice sounded like waves crashing against rocks on a beach. "What did you just say?"

"I said please don't tell anyone that you were here or you talked to me," she said softly. "It will be bad. For me."

He smiled. "I'll keep the secret on one condition."

"Anything," she admitted.

"That you talk to me when I come back."

"I don't know if I should do that," she said. "I just want to be left alone."

"For some reason I can't promise you that," he admitted. "Being in this house everyday is fucking with my head and you're the most interesting thing I've seen in a long time." He walked toward the door and turned the knob. "I won't tell anyone I was here or that I talked to you, but I will be back whether you speak to me or not." He walked out.

Nine dropped to her knees and exhaled. The entire time he'd been there, he had taken her breath away.

CHAPTER TWENTY NINE

"The time of life is short."
-William Shakespeare

The next few days Nine had something to look forward to and his name was Leaf Lincoln. He stood by his word and came into her room every night. So that she wouldn't get into trouble it was always after midnight when everyone else was asleep. Leaf did most of the talking but Nine would laugh or say a word or two so that he would know she was interested.

She was waiting on him to visit again when she heard screaming and bumping around upstairs. The house was solid and sound very rarely traveled unless the noise upstairs was extremely loud.

When she heard someone yell, "The CIA is coming! The CIA is coming to get me." She was startled.

The voice was faint before but now it was clear. The person was her mother. Afraid she would come into her room, Nine pushed her desk and chair in front of the door. She was not allowed to block access but she was willing to get in trouble to avoid Kelly. She walked backwards slowly and waited. Just as she expected the doorknob jiggled and her mother banged against the door heavily.

"The CIA is coming! The CIA is coming!"

Nine was smart enough to know who the CIA was but wasn't sure what they wanted from her mother if anything.

Shortly after Kelly's first knock and the attempt she made to get into Nine's room, she heard extra footsteps. Then it was her grandfather's angry voice that rocked her spirit. "What is all of this madness, Kelly?" Kerrick yelled. "What are you talking about now?"

"The CIA," Kelly continued. "They are coming to get me!"

"Honey, come back to bed," Avery said softly. "Everything will be fine."

"But they're coming to get me! I don't want them to get me," she sobbed. "Will you help me?"

"She's doing it again," Kerrick said harshly. His voice was heavy with irritation. "I thought you said it had stopped, Avery. You promised me that you would keep her mental issues under control.

"It did stop, father," Avery responded. "But something happened tonight and she snapped. I was in the bathroom and when I came out she was down here."

"I told you what I would do if this happened again. I was very clear. Unfortunately we'll have to keep her down here. We have company in the house and I don't want Justin and Corrine to see this."

Nine watched the door as if she were watching a movie. Although she couldn't see their actions, she could hear their voices. Before long Nine heard a dragging noise across the floor. It was her mother's body.

"Get off of me," Kelly screamed. "Leave me be!" Her mind alternated between thoughts. "And where is Paige? Where is my daughter? Who has my babies?"

"She left a long time ago," Avery said. His voice was heavy with sympathy and love. He did all he could to stop himself from crying.

A few seconds later Nine heard a door open and slam quickly thereafter. Kelly had been placed in a room across from Nine's. Now she was an inmate too. Kerrick had many rooms in his house, and many more in the basement. If he wanted to keep his entire family imprisoned he could and the world would never know.

"Let me out," Kelly screamed banging heavily on the door. "Please, father. Let me out."

Kerrick and Avery walked upstairs and Nine could hear their footsteps along with her father's soft crying. It was the first time Nine heard Avery weep and she wondered why he never cried for her. He was obsessed when it came to his wife and had little love left for his daughters.

When the melodrama ceased, Nine pulled the desk from the door and sat down on the bed. The sounds of her mother crying that the CIA was approaching covered the night. At first being alone in the basement bothered Nine. Mainly because she was forced to stay with her own thoughts. But what she wouldn't give to have noiselessness now.

The next day the same thing occurred with Kelly accept she was louder. She ranted on and on about the CIA. She yelled so long that her voice was hoarse and barely recognizable.

Each day Avery would beg Kerrick to let her out and each time he would say no. Avery even offered to move out of the home if Kerrick would provide the first few months' rent. Still Kerrick refused because he knew it would be a few weeks, if not days, before they returned for help. Besides, with Kelly's mental condition deteriorating he couldn't risk someone finding out about the incest that plagued the Prophet family.

As if Nine didn't resent her mother enough, because she was downstairs too, it had been weeks since she'd seen Leaf. There were too many people going in the basement for him to visit. She was wrong to look forward to seeing him, knowing nothing in her life was promised, but it didn't stop how she felt.

The next morning when Nine woke up she was enveloped in silence. Although her wish had been granted about not wanting to hear her mother's voice, now she was frightened. It was too quiet. So she popped the lock, crept to the engine room and into the ducts. She crawled into almost every vent and it appeared everyone was gone.

Emboldened, she crawled out of the vent and walked toward the living room. Her bare feet sank into the plush cream carpet as she approached the ceiling to floor window. She pushed open the curtains just in time to see her mother being taken out of the house kicking and screaming. There in the driveway stood Avery, Kerrick, Victoria, Fran and a few people standing by a black van she didn't recognize. For some reason her heart rocked in her chest.

She picked up the edge of her pajamas so she wouldn't trip and rushed back to her bedroom. Something odd was going on.

An hour later there was a soft knock at the door. She wanted it more than anything to be Leaf. Nine hopped out of bed and stood in front of the door as she waited for her visitor. When it opened, her father stood on the other side. She was majorly disappointed. What did he want?

"Your mother isn't coming back," he said as gigantic tears rolled down his face. "But I'm not sad anymore. He killed her and I'm happy for her. She doesn't have to hurt any longer."

Nine stood in place, not knowing what he wanted her to say. She didn't know either of them and she despised him for involving her in their business.

"I can tell as I stand in front of you that you hate me. And you have that right. I loved your mother so hard that I didn't have enough love for my girls." He wiped the tears from his face with his sleeve and Nine noticed he had a gun. "I did a horrible job in this life, Nine."

Nine backed against the wall thinking he would shoot her.

"I don't have anything to give you. So I offer my life instead." He raised the gun that dangled in his hand, placed it to his temple and pulled the trigger.

Bone matter slapped against the rim of the door and splattered against her face. She observed the colorful gruesome scene in awe. She examined the brain tissue that was slapped against the wall and the white part of his eye that sat at her foot.

A rush that Nine never experienced coursed through her body as she studied the scene. And she would replay it in her mind for the rest of her life.

CHAPTER TWENTY-ONE
NINE

"Doomsday is near; die all, die merrily."
-William Shakespeare

Nine's heart hardened ever since her father murdered himself. She was left with thoughts of Kerrick and how everything was his entire fault. Who was the man she called grandfather really? What had he gone through which made him mentally abuse his family? It didn't matter. She made up in her mind that she would spend her life getting revenge against him. And she didn't care how long it would take.

And then there was the problem with Alice. No matter what she did, this monster refused to leave her alone.

Nine was bent over on her desk with her rear in the air like she had been many times before. Her cousin and Hector were lying on the floor beneath her eying her body while they made love. When Alice observed Hector no longer performing because he was enamored with Nine's body, she grew insanely jealous.

"Get the fuck off me," she said pushing him by the shoulders. "You are so worthless. I can't believe I am going to marry you."

He rolled off of her and they both stood up and pulled up their clothes.

"But what did I do this time?" he asked.

"You choose to eye this bitch when you have the benefit of me!" she paused. "Your belt, Hector," she said holding her hand out, palm up. "Give it to me now!"

"What are you going to do?" he asked hoping she wasn't going to hit him.

"Punish this bitch for looking at you too hard. It's obvious if you disconnected from me it was all her fault."

"Alice, please," he smiled hoping she'd calm down. "Let's just go upstairs and eat."

"Give…me…your…belt," she demanded wiggling her fingers. "Now!"

Not trying to anger the woman who could take her money away and ruin his life in the process, he slowly pulled the buckle until the belt was hanging at his side. He took a look at Nine whose hands were still on the table, as she was faced in the opposite direction. She hadn't done a thing wrong. As weird as it was, considering he was a part of Alice's antics too, he still felt sorry for her.

Alice snatched the belt and hit Nine so hard on the rear with the buckle that her flesh ripped open. The metal attachment dug into her skin and caused her to bleed immediately. Alice was so delusional that she felt she was in the right. Furthermore she had no intentions on stopping until Nine begged for mercy.

But after the fourth whack Nine had refused to budge. So Alice doubled the lashes hoping she'd relent. Still Nine did not flinch. The flesh of her right cheek bled even more but what Nine lacked was reaction.

When Alice walked around to look at Nine's expression she was smiling. Frightened, Alice dropped the belt and said, "Fuck this bitch. Let's get out of here. I'm getting tired of smelling this whore anyway."

When Alice closed the door, Nine stood in the middle of the floor and laughed crazily.

A few days later Fran sat on Nine's chair and observed her while she was sitting on the edge of the bed. Nine was different but Fran couldn't figure out how. "Are you sad about your father?"

"No."

"Are you going to talk to me?" she took a large gulp of the whiskey in the small paper bag she was clutching. "Or are you going to remain silent forever?"

Nine focused on the floor. Slowly her head rolled up until she was looking into Fran's eyes. "What would make my father kill himself? In all of my books, including the bible you speak about, it says that suicide is the worst sin."

"You have your opinion and that's great. But unless you've lived everyone else's life, you should never judge."

Nine swallowed. "What happened to my grandfather? To make him so evil and abuse his family?"

Fran sighed. "I don't know a lot but I'll tell you what he told me during happier times. Your grandfather was born in Zimbabwe. He was in love with a woman very much, a woman that neither your grandmother or me could ever hold a candle to. Her name was Thandi. She was murdered for something he did to make money that he never spoke of. But," she paused, "prior to that he was forced to kill his parents for a militia group in Africa. He didn't tell me much about what went on during his time with them, but I think it changed the course of how he viewed people. Of how he viewed himself." She paused. "I will never forget something he did say about that group. He said that he wanted to fight for them when he lost his parents but they told him no. Because he wasn't hard enough. So he became a monster instead."

Nine considered what Fran said but her mind was made up. "When I am ready, I will kill him."

Fran looked deeply into her eyes. "I know."

"Can I talk to you about something else?"

Fran swallowed the rest of her liquor and tossed the bottle in the bucket. "Just ask."

"Lately I've been having the desire to…to…touch myself," she stuttered. "And I don't know why."

Fran moved uneasily in her seat. She always knew this moment would come and she hoped she'd have something good to say. But she didn't. Instead she rubbed her hands together and her eyes darted around the room.

Finally she cleared her throat and said, "When you get this feeling, what are you thinking about?"

Now it was Nine who was uncomfortable. She didn't want to say how she was aroused by thoughts of violence or the bad things she read in her books. Or that the way Leaf rubs his hands down his thighs when he's sitting down makes her horny. Anyway he was not supposed to be in her room and every time Fran asked if he had visited she would lie. "I don't really think about anything."

Fran nodded her head up and down. "Okay, okay, let me tell you about your body then. She stood up and released one of the buttons on her soiled maid uniform.

"What are you doing?" Nine asked confused. "I don't want you to—"

"Just sit down there," Fran ordered. She pulled her uniform off until it was lying at her feet. She stood in front of Nine wearing a graying white bra and purple panties. What Nine noticed immediately was the scar on her belly.

"This is the scar Kerrick gave me," Fran said rubbing her hand over the old wound. "Remember the story I told you? About not being able to have kids?"

Nine nodded.

Fran didn't wait for Nine to say anything; instead she sat down on the chair and removed her panties. Nine could smell the sour scent of Fran's vagina spraying through the room. The brown hair on her vagina was speckled with gray hairs. Fran looked up at Nine and said, "I'm going to show you how to make yourself feel good so that you will never have to depend on a man."

Nine's eyes looked as if they would pop out of her head. "O…okay," she stuttered.

Fran pulled the lips of her vagina apart with her index finger and middle finger. The flesh of her pink vagina glistened and her tiny clit was tucked backwards as if it were trying to hide.

"This is where you would allow a man to enter you," Fran said pointing at her hole. "You can be stimulated if he takes the time to learn your body but if not you won't have much pleasure here."

"Stimulated?"

"Yes. I'm talking about an orgasm." Fran pointed at her clit. "Now by rubbing this repeatedly it will stiffen and you will reach one. Do it as much as you want and you will have many." To demonstrate, she spread her legs wider and rubbed her clit. It hardened and before long it stuck out like a tiny button.

Fran, under the influence of alcohol, forgot where she was and she continued to rub it as she escaped into the moment.

Nine never took her eyes off of Fran and she watched her juice up as if she were urinating on herself.

Before long Fran moaned out an orgasm and bit down on her bottom lip. Because she was not clean the room held a rotten odor. It didn't bother Nine too much. A similar odor came from her own body when she wasn't hosed regularly.

What her family didn't know was that since Leaf came into her life, she had started sneaking showers when everyone in the house was gone. She wanted to be clean for him. During these times she would pretend to be not only a member of the Prophet family but its leader.

After Fran reached an orgasm she saw Nine looking at her as if she were a movie. "I'm sorry about that,"

Fran said jumping up and sliding on her panties, followed by her uniform. "It was important for me to show you how to please yourself." She cleared her throat. "Because if you can satisfy yourself, a man can't have control over you. What's the second rule of seduction?"

"Control your body, mind and soul and you will rule the world."

"Good," she smiled.

"Well let me go," she paused, "I'll be back later if I can."

When she left Nine quickly removed her nightgown. She lie back in the bed and rubbed herself the way Fran had taught her. She couldn't believe the feeling that came over her body as she moved her fingers briskly. She did it five more times that night and she didn't think about food, her parents or the condition of her life. She was forced into a coma-like sleep.

Fran was right.

She felt powerful.

Leaf sat on the chair across from Nine smiling at her. He had been spending more time with her when he was able, and the two of them built a stronger bond. Since there was so much secrecy surrounding the Prophets they avoided certain topics like who he was and who she was. And as a result, they didn't know they were cousins.

"I bought you something," he said taking a brown paper bag out of his North Face book bag. He opened it and handed her a honey bun. Although he wanted her to have the treat that wasn't the real purpose of giving it to her. He wanted to find out how isolated she really was from the outside world. "I got it from 7-Eleven."

"7-Eleven?" she repeated.

"Yeah," he said getting his answer. She had no clues about the world outside. "It's a convenience store."

"Well what is it?" she asked looking at the white iced bun through the plastic.

"Eat it and find out."

She pulled and tugged at the plastic wrap but it didn't open quickly enough. "Here, let me get it for you," he gently took it out of her hand and ripped it. When it was open he handed it back. "There you go."

Nine snatched the bun and took her first bite. Her eyes opened and she looked at him excitedly. A smile spread across her face and she started giggling and food hung out of the corners of her mouth. It was the most amazing thing she had ever eaten in her life. "Oh, my goodness, it's like heaven."

Her excitement over the honey bun caused him to laugh too. "I take it you like it."

"I love it," she said with her mouth full as she took bite after bite fearing someone would take it away. "Do you have another?"

"Not right now," he said wishing he had bought two.

Leaf had given chick's gifts in the past. Purses, expensive trips and the like. But this was the only time he got enjoyment that had nothing to do with sex.

Nine sat on the bed Indian style and devoured the honey bun until it had vanished before his eyes. She smiled at him the entire time. "Thank you," she said when she was done before licking her fingers. "Thank you so much for thinking of me."

Leaf looked at her pretty face and grew angry. Why was this obviously intelligent and beautiful girl living in a basement? Why was he able to make her day with a honey bun? There was so much in the world to see and she was being kept from it.

In the past he promised himself he wasn't going to pry but he was prepared to break it now. But he heard his name being called faintly upstairs. If he heard it in the basement it meant they were calling him loudly.

Nine's eyes widened and she was fearful again. "You'd better go," she said in a whisper. "They can't find you down here."

He moved quickly not because he was scared for himself. He moved swiftly because he was starting to care about Nine and he was worried for her. "I'll be back tonight," he said before leaving.

"Can you bring me one of those honey buns if you do?" she asked.

He winked. "You got it, mami. Anything you want."

When he left Nine sat on the edge of the bed and considered what she was feeling in her chest. It was a squeezing sensation that seemed to rush to the pit of her stomach. It always intensified whenever Leaf was around. Was this the emotion Fran warned her about? The one she read about constantly in Shakespeare's books?

Was number Nine in love?

Leaf didn't walk directly into the living room from the entrance leading out of the basement. Instead he went out the back of the house and came around the front and rung the doorbell. He was trying to be sure that no one knew he was in the basement.

The moment he pushed the doorbell Kerrick snatched him inside as if he were in the Matrix. His expression was tight and when he was pushed into the den, there were three men who Leaf didn't recognize.

Justin was present too. Justin was sitting on the sofa with a glass of scotch in his hand. He looked as if he'd seen a ghost.

Leaf's heart thumped because Justin, his father, was never upset. He was cool and easy going which is where Leaf got his disposition.

"Autumn, this is Riley, Mox and Jameson," Kerrick said interrupting Leaf's gaze on Justin. "They've been protecting me for years and now they will be protecting you."

He frowned. "Protecting me for what? I thought we had nothing to worry about. And that I was going to turn myself in next week to answer to the charges."

"Son, that girl you killed is the daughter of an important man," Justin said.

Leaf didn't doubt that. She was always dressed nice and wore the finest perfume. "What does that mean?" He looked at all of them. "Who's her father?" he asked.

"His name is Johnny Gates. The girl you killed was Chloe Gates."

CHAPTER TWENTY-TWO
KERRICK

"Play out the play."
-William Shakespeare

Kerrick met Gates in an oblong three-story house outside of Baltimore. The back and side of the property was plain and unpainted and Kerrick was surprised because for a man of Gate's caliber, the home was nothing to look at. Gates had told Kerrick that he lived in the rundown establishment but he knew that was not the case. Gates did not trust him, so he did not invite him to where he rested his head.

With serious business at hand, Kerrick, Riley, Mox and Jameson were led into the tenement and outside of the back by two armed men. Eventually they found themselves in a vast patio, one hundred and fifty feet in length. It was paved with white marble and decorated with imitation plants around the perimeter. Gates was building the house for his seventeen-year-old daughter who never got to see it because she was murdered by Leaf.

Kerrick scanned the patio for his guest. He saw Gates sitting at a rusted table that only sat two. Three of his men stood behind him and a tray with a silver and gold teapot dressed with pink flowers sat in the middle.

Gates waved Kerrick over with a smile that was as lifeless as the condition of the building.

Kerrick strolled toward him as if all of his worries were already over. His five thousand dollar navy blue suit swayed as he moved with the wind. Before sitting down, he unbuttoned his jacket, took a seat and crossed his legs. His men stood strong behind him as ready to protect him as they did when he was a young goon on the Baltimore block.

"Tea?" Gates asked politely.

"No," Kerrick responded. "I never touch the stuff. Not good for the heart." He beat his chest once before putting his hands back into his lap.

"Well I hope you don't mind if I do." Gates poured himself some and took his time placing cream and sugar inside of his cup. "My wife bought this set for my daughter. I don't know why she thought Chloe would like such a feminine thing. She was more rough around the edges, just like me."

"Where is your wife now?" he looked around.

"With my twin daughters in Mumbai. They'll be back tomorrow."

Kerrick sat back in his seat and crossed his legs. "So why am I here? Clearly there are other things to discuss outside of your daughter's teapot." He paused. "What do you want to help smooth over your loss."

"Your grandson murdered my daughter. And I understand that this morning you turned him into the authorities to answer questions in the case."

"I did."

"Well we both know he will get off for the charges. Witnesses are already saying that my daughter was the aggressor."

"Exactly, which is why I don't understand why we are here. Autumn will be exonerated and it won't bring your daughter back. Why can't we be men about it and let things go? What are you asking in terms of finances?"

Gates took a sip of tea with his baby finger extended. "Two million dollars."

Kerrick felt the price was steep but he would pay it if it meant his family would be okay. "And what does that buy me?"

"Your wife, yourself and your business will remain untouched."

"And what about my grandson?"

"You know I cannot allow him to live," he sat the teacup down. "Out of respect for you I waited to speak to you before putting a bullet in his head. Once you leave here my charity is over."

Kerrick's jaw twitched. "Even if you wanted to kill him he's protected twenty-four hours a day."

"There are always ways."

"If you touch my grandson there will be war."

"This is war now."

Kerrick stood up, and stole a few moments to button his jacket. "I do not make many promises but I will make you this one. During this battle I will make sure you remain alive. So you can live long enough to see everything you love die."

CHAPTER TWENTY-THREE
KERRICK

"Company, villainous company, hath been the spoil of me."
-William Shakespeare

A few days passed since Kerrick visited Gates and the Prophet family had not been the same since. Leaf had beaten the charges when video footage sent by one of the students caught Chloe pulling an illegal handgun on Leaf. But winning his case didn't mean party time for the Prophets either. For starters it took fifty men to protect him as he was lead out of the courtroom. But it would take many more to keep him alive.

Nine lie down in the duct leading to the living room. She was peering through the vent and watching Kerrick argue with Leaf. Her mind rambled. Why was Kerrick so protective of a kid who was not his blood?

"I don't understand what's going on," Leaf said as he paced the floor. "My father's not answering the phone. My mother's not at the office and she's not reaching out to me either. Can you be honest with me?"

Kerrick was seated calmly on the sofa with his legs crossed. "Autumn…"

"Leaf," he yelled.

Kerrick closed his eyes in frustration. The killer in him wanted to yank the kid by his vocal chords and whisper stories of the boys he killed for less in his ear. But the grandfather in him was getting old and tiring of violence. With all that said, at the moment anyway, his patience was water thin.

"We tried to offer Gates money to let you live but he declined. The only thing he wants is your blood. So as much as I hate to say it, you can't leave this house."

Leaf walked over to the recliner and plopped down. "But where are my parents?"

"Somewhere safe. I offered them one of the rooms here but they have something to take care of first before they can come back." He uncrossed his legs. "You have full reign of the house, the only thing I ask is that you refrain from entering the basement."

"You said that before," he exhaled not wanting to stay away from Nine.

"And I'll say it again," Kerrick said firmly. "Everything in that basement belongs to me and I don't want you touching it. You disobey any order of my command and you're on the streets. Left to protect yourself. If that's what you want try me."

It was midnight. Nine was sitting on the bed hoping that Leaf would not heed her grandfather's warnings by ceasing his visits. She had gotten use to his attention and craved it to live through her days. He was her escape.

When she heard someone approach the door, she popped up and stood in the middle of the floor. She just knew it would be Leaf. A smile spread across her face and she couldn't wait to read him Shakespeare, which thanks to her he had grown to love.

But when the door opened she was devastated when she saw it was Kerrick instead. He was surprised to see her standing in front of the door but he was more surprised to see her smiling. She lived in his basement and barely ate. What did she have to be so happy about? "Why are you grinning girl?"

She shook her head from left to right first. "No reason, grandfather. Just something I read in one of my books."

Kerrick stepped closer. "What did you read that got you feeling all goofy?"

"Something Shakespeare wrote," she lied. "Nothing serious."

He looked her over with a slow examination. She was changing and he wanted to know how. "You aren't entertaining people down here are you? Because I warned you what would happen if you did."

Nine felt sweat drops roll from her underarms and cruise down the sides of her body. "No, grandfather."

"Because I don't want anybody in here," he said touching her shoulder roughly. "Ever! Now that your parents are gone you are my sole responsibility. And I take that very seriously."

"I understand, grandfather. What about Alice? And her friend?" she paused. "Are they allowed to visit?"

His forehead crinkled. "She's the only one outside of Fran who is allowed in here. No one else. Are we clear?"

Nine sighed. If he had said Alice was not allowed she was planning to tell him about all of her freaky antics. Instead she kept it to herself. "We're clear, grandfather."

"Good. Now where is Fran?" he asked looking around her room.

"I don't know," she said softly, almost toddler like. "The last time I spoke with her she said she was going to the liquor store. And that was earlier in the day."

"Well when you see her tell her to come see me."

Before letting Kerrick exit Nine decided to see if what she'd been learning, with her seduction skills, had been working. What better person to try it on than her grandfather? But she was afraid that he would see right through her and punish her that night. But in an effort to be free, it was worth a try.

He was about to leave until she muttered, "Grandfather."

He turned around. "Yes."

"You look handsome today," she said.

He grinned and forced it to melt away. "What do you know about handsome?" He tried to prevent another smile from infiltrating his face but it was difficult.

"I see a lot of men on the pages of my books but none are as handsome as you."

Upon hearing her response Kerrick stormed out of the room without another word. She felt as if her plan had backfired and she wouldn't be surprised if he beat her later for her insolence. So she sat on the edge of the bed and tried to stay up. But her willpower was not as strong and eventually she dosed off.

When she woke up the next morning and saw someone leaving her room she figured it was Fran. She popped up and her feet slapped against the hardwood floor. There, in the middle of her room sat her chair. And in the center of it was a gorgeous red dress with little pink hearts around the neckline.

Her grandfather bought the gift.

She grinned. Her seduction was working. And yet she was just getting started.

CHAPTER TWENTY-FOUR
NINE

"I dote on his very absence."
-William Shakespeare

It had been a week since Nine had seen Fran and even longer since she'd seen Leaf. She knew he was in the house because she crawled through the ducts everyday to see him eat breakfast, just to get a look at him. She guessed her grandfather's threats had worked on him after all and she was devastated. She never took Leaf as soft but now she knew better.

Everyday she played make believe using the outfit Kerrick had bought for her. She pretended she was allowed to leave the house and had a party to attend. Although it was beautiful, it didn't feel as special without someone to show it too. Fran was right. Love was dumb and a waste of her time.

As the days passed Nine started to believe that she would never see Fran again. This was the longest she'd ever gone without seeing her. Because Fran knew she was the only one who cared about feeding Nine, she couldn't believe she would lead her astray for so long.

The only light in her tunnel was that suddenly Kerrick had taken an interest in seeing that Nine stayed nourished. And he brought her good food too, steak, fried chicken, mashed potatoes. Whatever they ate upstairs, the girl downstairs enjoyed too.

Still…where was her dear Fran?

She was sitting on the edge of the bed looking out into the room when the door opened. She didn't look at it. There was no use in getting her hopes high. Instead she remained frozen thinking that it was either Kerrick or Alice. But when she saw Leaf on the other side holding a brown paper bag she was surprised.

"Hey," he said coming in and closing the door behind himself. "I snuck out of the house and bought you something you may like." He raised the bag in the air and she knew her honey bun was inside.

"I don't want it," she said with an attitude. "I ate already."

He pulled a chair up to the bed and sat the bag on the floor. He placed his elbows on his knees and looked over at her. His right leg shook rapidly as he tried to figure out what to say. "Look, I gotta lot of shit going on in my life right now. And I didn't—"

"Why are you telling me this?" she asked cutting him off. "You don't owe me an explanation. You're not even supposed to be in here. Just go."

He looked down at the floor and thought carefully about what to say next. Leaf was a spoiled kid. A kid who got everything he wanted and yet he couldn't understand why the strange girl downstairs intrigued him so much. He wanted to get up, walk out and yell fuck you, but he couldn't move.

"I'm sorry," he pleaded with her. "I was told not to come down here so I didn't. Normally I don't listen to what people say which is why I'm here now. Can you forgive me, Nine? Please?"

Nine jumped up and shuffled toward the door. She pulled it open and looked down at her feet. She didn't like feeling emotions for Leaf but it was far too late. Fran told her to never place herself in a situation where her emotions ruled and yet she had done it anyway.

Instead of walking out he stood up and closed the door. He yanked Nine toward him and forced her back against the door. She was so grateful that today was shower day because he was the closest he had ever been.

Leaf placed his lips against hers and his tongue snaked inside of her mouth. Nine's body felt activated and the hairs on the surface of her skin rose.

Having zero experience with kissing she decided it would be best if she allowed him to take the lead. Every time she felt his tongue stroke against hers her clitoris vibrated. Before long she found the rhythm and was able to kiss him like a pro.

This must be the *passion* Shakespeare talked about in his books.

When her body was already on a rollercoaster, Leaf lifted her up so that her legs wrapped around his waist. With one hand he quickly unfastened his jeans and removed his stiff penis. In all of the excitement he poked her a few times in the wrong position trying to find her wetness.

But his persistence wouldn't allow him to stop and for that he was rewarded. He eased into her body until her plushness engulfed him. She moaned at first and he realized what he was doing. Making love to a virgin, something he never did before. Considerate of her feelings he asked, "Are you okay? Do you want me to stop?"

"Please don't, "she responded. "I've dreamed about this day for a long time."

Before long she felt a sensation she never felt with another person before. It started at her clit and spread throughout her entire body. Tears fell down her face because she never knew someone else could make her feel so magical. A few more seconds and Leaf was right behind her as he also reached an orgasm.

When he was done they kissed for another minute and he gently picked her up and walked her over to the bed. When she was seated, he took off his white t-shirt and wiped his penis. It was red.

"Are you sure you're okay? This is a lot of blood." he responded really concerned. He balled the shirt up and stuffed it in his pocket.

"I'm fine," she smiled while trying to stop her trembling legs. "Don't worry about me. I've had worse happen."

He didn't like the sound of that. "I don't know what this is between us but I want you to know that you're safe with me."

"Thank you, that means a lot," she smiled. She looked down at the floor next to the chair. "Is that my honey bun?" The smile he loved reappeared. "I want it now."

"I bet you do," he joked.

"What can I say, I built up an appetite." She opened the bag and tore into the treat. "And I want to do what we just did again. As many times as you want to," she asked as if they were playing a game instead of making love.

"As good as you feel, we can do it everyday."

Nine was lying in the bed face up with her mind on Leaf. He left her not even an hour earlier when her door opened again. This time it was Fran holding a bottle of whiskey in one hand and a gun in the other. "Get up and come with me," she said as her voice slurred.

A few minutes later they were outside, in the place where Fran taught her how to shoot. Fran was standing behind her as Nine was aiming at the tree. Her hand shook because she was afraid. Over the months Fran's alcohol habit had reached a dangerous level. And she had a feeling that guns and liquor didn't mix.

"Why are you shaking?" Fran asked. "Shoot!"

Nine pulled the trigger and missed her target.

"Shoot again!" She yelled in her ear.

Nine complied but missed.

"And again, and again and again until you learn to love gunfire." She poured what was left of the whiskey in her mouth and tossed the bottle on the ground.

Nine didn't want to shoot. She wanted to talk to Fran and be there for her. She wanted to hug her and tell her that whatever she was going through she would be okay. And that she was the strongest woman she'd known. She wanted to tell her about her first sexual experience. Above all she wanted to tell Fran that she loved her. Something she'd never done before.

When Fran fell on the ground Nine dropped to the cool grass with her. She crawled next to Fran's body, placed her head in her lap and rubbed her hair. "Fran, what's wrong?" a tear rolled down her cheek. "Talk to me. Please."

The moon lit up her sad face and Nine could see that she was crying too. "I've wasted my life, Nine. My entire life has been a joke. The only thing I'm proud of is you."

"But it's never too late, Fran. Right?"

"It's over for me. I should've never left Money Mouse for your grandfather."

"Why did you?"

She sighed. "Because Kerrick knew me. He knew the ugly side of me and still he stayed around. I'm just figuring out now that the real me wasn't worth much anyway so I got what I deserved. A monster."

When Fran was forcefully pulled out of Nine's arms she thought she was dreaming. She wasn't. Kerrick yanked Fran by her hair and when she was on her feet, he delivered a swift blow to her face, which brought her to her knees.

Remembering the gun, Fran crawled toward it but Kerrick grabbed her by the ankles. Nine was about to help Fran out until she yelled, "Nine, go back into the house!" Her eyes pleaded with Nine not to make the mistake of her lifetime. "Now is not the time. Now go!"

"You shouldn't even be out here," Kerrick growled, remembering his grandchild was present. "Get back inside. I'll deal with you later!"

Nine took one last look at Fran as she ran toward the mansion. She could only imagine what Kerrick had in store for the woman she had grown to love. When she was in her room she prayed to the God Fran talked about and asked for mercy for Fran's soul.

CHAPTER TWENTY-FIVE
NINE

"The weakest kind of fruit drops earliest to the ground."
-William Shakespeare

Nine sat in the middle of the room. In short spurts she held her breath before exhaling again. She had to do something to get her mind off of the look in Fran's eyes as Kerrick was preparing to beat the life out of her. Something told Nine she would never see her again and that fucked with her head.

The next morning came soon enough and Fran had not come to her. Surprisingly when the door opened it was Leaf.

She looked away from him and focused on her fingers that were still grimy from the soil on the ground from the last time she saw Fran. She felt awful about being happy when Fran's world had crumbled down. She didn't deserve love with Fran gone.

"How you doing?" he asked standing in the doorway. Nine's body was present but she wouldn't look at him. "Can I get you anything? I heard about the maid. I know ya'll were cool."

"What did you hear about her?" Nine asked, curious to know what happened.

"Just that she got into a fight with Kerrick."

Nine thought about the lessons Fran gave her about life. And how she warned her against love and feeling for another person. Perhaps if Fran hadn't loved her grandfather so much she wouldn't be...possibly...dead.

Nine pushed the thought out of her mind. It was too big to hold. Besides with Fran gone who would love her? Who would care about her? Who would teach her about the ways of the world? Nobody. She feared it would be nobody. Ever again!

Slowly her head rose until she was staring directly into Leaf's eyes. "Never come here again. If you do I will kill you."

Leaf stopped in his place and stood directly in front of her. He frowned but tried to remove the anger from his expression. Did she just say she would kill him? "Did you just threaten me?"

"What do you think you know about me that would make you think my words are a threat instead of a promise?" her question was as cold as an iceberg in Alaska. "I showed you what I wanted you to see. Nothing less nothing more." A tear rolled down her face as she released venom to somebody who didn't deserve it. "I'm locked down here for a reason, Leaf. Now leave my room or I will be forced to show you my other side."

Leaf felt she was hurting, for what he didn't know. But he wasn't the type to stand and accept abuse either. His patience was limited and Nine spent all of his nerves. So he walked out without another word.

Two days passed and Nine remained in the same spot until the door slowly opened. She was still hopeful that Fran was okay and that she would come back, but it was Alice who's face she saw.

Alice crawled into the room and closed the door behind her. She stood in front of the door with an artificial smile on her face and her hands clasped behind her back.

Nine looked at her briefly, before looking down at her fingers again.

"You look bad," Alice said looking over her head at the desk. "And judging by the smell of the spoiled food on your dresser, I take it you haven't eaten either."

Nine remained silent. Her blood boiled under the surface. If Alice said the wrong thing it could be dangerous.

"I realize you're mad but I'm here with news," she said taking one more step. "I just wanted to let you know that your precious maid called."

Now Alice had her complete attention. She parted her lips slowly. They were so sticky because she hadn't spoken, eaten or drank anything. "What"— she licked her lips—"did she say?"

"To tell you hello," she smiled. "If she calls again I'll let you know." She shrugged and walked out of the door.

Inspired by Fran being well, she rose up from her seat. Her legs felt like worms under her body due to sitting down for so long. She moved as quickly as she could to the table, grabbed the cup of water and downed it all. When she was done she paced the room and wandered what happened to Fran and when she would be coming back.

After awhile Nine convinced herself that Fran would be back at any minute and she felt bad for threatening Leaf. If she hadn't been so mean she would have his company while she waited on Fran's return.

But three more days passed and still Fran didn't show her face. Her grandmother took over the responsibility of feeding her but she was cold as usual when she brought the meals. Nine was finding it harder to sit with herself again due to worrying so much about Fran. And when she was so ill her heart ached Alice came back into the room.

She stood in front of the door and clasped her hands in front of her. "I'm sorry, Nine, but Fran called again. She told me to tell you that she's never coming back. Oh, and that she hates you and hopes you die here."

Nine's heart ached and she didn't believe her. Why would Fran say she hated her when all she showed was love? "She wouldn't say that," Nine proclaimed. "She would never say that to me."

"It's up to you whether you want to believe me or not," Alice shrugged. "I'm just bringing you the news."

For the next week Alice placed Nine under repeated torture. Telling her that Fran was on her way only for her to never show up. Later telling her that Fran wished she were dead but then claiming she loved her in the same breath. Nine was growing colder and her hate for her cousin had reached severe levels.

On the final day Alice came into the room with hopes of altering Nine's mood she was met with something else.

"Fran was on the phone again," she said standing at the door. "She said she might come back if you promise you'll kill yourself a few days later. She said that would be the only way she'd know you love her."

Nine stood up and took a step toward Alice. This frightened her because in the past Nine had never been bold enough to look directly into her eyes. Slowly her lips parted and she said, "Why do you poke the monster? When you know it can eat you alive?"

The smirk disappeared from Alice's face and she hustled out of the room backwards. The next day the door didn't open but an envelope was slid under the doorway. Nine reluctantly walked over to it knowing it would be some sort of torture technique from Alice. But when she opened the envelope, and removed a picture, it caused her heartbeat to create a new rhythm.

Lying in a shallow grave was Fran, whose face was speckled with dirt. Her eyes were closed and it was obvious that she was dead.

Alice, knowing where all the dead bodies went, dug up Fran's body just to get the picture.

On the back of the picture was a note, handwritten by Alice. "My monster is bigger than yours."

Nine's body plopped to the ground and she sobbed her last cry. When she emerged she would be a person everyone who wronged her should fear.

CHAPTER TWENTY-SIX
NINE

"Off with his head!"
-William Shakespeare

It was after midnight and the Prophet mansion appeared to be embedded in a darkness that Nine had never felt before. The sounds of the lightning storm outside made her uneasy.

She was so emotionally torn over Fran's murder that at first she thought her mind was playing tricks on her when she heard glass breaking in the basement. The only window downstairs was over the washing machine and dryer. Something was off.

Carefully Nine crept to her bedroom door, popped the lock like she always did. She pulled the door open and immersed herself into deeper darkness. Once outside of her room she eased toward the engine room without needing an inch of light. She knew the inner workings of the mansion like no other, and would use it to her advantage as she determined who was in their home.

Nine crawled through the ducts and peered through vent after vent until she discovered what she knew existed…unwanted strangers in the Prophet mansion.

She spotted them in the foyer and realized she had to think quickly. She overheard the conversations in the mansion. She knew they were hit men sent for Leaf. If she screamed Leaf may run out and get killed instantly. So she had to be calculating. She had to be smart.

Believing they were there to kill Autumn, she rushed toward the exit of the duct. The edge of her nightgown got snagged onto the vent and tore. Time was not on her side. She would have to do this chore in the nude.

Stew, who worked for Gates, had one order. To kill Leaf, along with anybody who stood in his way. So under the cover of night and during a lightning storm, he successfully broke into the Prophet Mansion through the basement. His partner Roland had already gone his separate way to see if he could find the young killer first. Although both men would be paid handsomely for their services, who ever actually spilled Leaf's blood would be paid extra.

Choosing the back stairwell of the mansion, Stew walked slowly down the corridor. His gun was aimed in front of him as he prepared to murder whomever came first. He was so focused on what was before him that he didn't feel Nine prowling behind him. She was naked due to her nightgown being stuck in the vent but that wouldn't stop her murder game. She had been a secret of the mansion for so long that she was as quiet as the walls. He would never see her coming.

Stew almost made it to Kelly's old bedroom until Nine snuck behind him, slapped her hand over his mouth and sliced his throat. His body went limp and she wiggled to the floor with him, so that he wouldn't make a thud when he dropped.

One down. One more to go.

Roland couldn't find his way around the house as easily as Stew. The darkness was unkind and he bumped into several surfaces. His knees and hip were on fire.

The crackling of thunder forced fear into his heart and he was secretly hoping that Stew did the job so that he wouldn't have too. His plan was to tell Gates that he had looked for Leaf just as hard but was unsuccessful.

He decided to move back toward the kitchen and hang out in that area until Stew did the dirty work. But the moment he dipped inside of it he saw Nine standing before him, naked as the day she was born.

Although he hadn't planned on killing at all after he made his decision to let Stew do his thing, surely he could murder her and then say that she was trying to get in his way, when Gates asked how he contributed. But her body was so sexy that he decided to take her into one of the bathrooms, rape her and then steal her life afterwards. He was a two minute brother so a few seconds with a woman like that was all he needed.

"Please don't hurt me," Nine whispered with her hands raised by her sides. "I was just getting some juice. I won't tell anybody you're here. I promise. Just don't kill me."

Roland licked his dark smoker's lips and approached her. "If you come with me I won't hurt you," he said looking at her succulent breasts. Feeling unworried by her presence, he tucked the gun in his jeans and grabbed her by the arm.

Nine wiggled out of his hold, grabbed the handle of the knife, which sat tucked between her ass cheeks and slit his throat. She was able to control his yell like she had Stew's because Roland was led by lust.

Although he was dying he grabbed a hold of Nine's arm and she stabbed him again in the chest. Finally he dropped to the kitchen floor. Worried he would rise she cradled him, and stabbed him repeatedly until the cream marble floors were slick with blood. The whites of his eyes were lifeless and it was then that she realized he was dead.

When the light came on Nine jumped up preparing to kill more. Instead she was looking at Kerrick and Leaf who had guns aimed in her direction. Nine dropped the knife and raised her hands in the air. The only part of her body that wasn't red with blood was her eyes.

"Nine? Is that you?" Kerrick asked as they lowered their weapons.

"I killed him," she said breathing heavily. Her breasts rose and fell. "He broke in with the other man in the hallway upstairs. He's dead too."

CHAPTER TWENTY-SEVEN
NINE

"I am poor as Job, my lord, but not so patient."
-William Shakespeare

Nine paced the floor in front of the door in her bedroom. Out of everything she'd been through, losing Fran, her first sexual encounter and even killing two intruders, today was the most nervous day of her life. She would finally be meeting members of The Prophet family.

She looked down at the dress Kerrick bought her. It wasn't as new anymore as it was when he had first given it to her but it was the nicest thing she owned. She hoped it would suffice.

Not wanting to keep her grandfather waiting any longer she opened the door and made a right into the engine room. Her plan was to go through the ducts and see what the family was up to. What conversations were taking place behind her back. That is until she remembered she'd been given an invitation to join Kerrick upstairs and sneaking through the ducts was no longer necessary.

Nine took a deep breath and crept up the stairwell. Her bare feet nestled into the floorboards as she made her way to the dining room. When she made it upstairs she was staring at a sea of beautiful people standing around the dining room table. Her eyes bulged as she witnessed the spread of food in front of them. A whole turkey, mashed potatoes, green beans and apple pie were just a few of the treats waiting for her.

Members of the family wanted to know where Nine had been hidden. Outside of Victoria, Alice and Leaf no one knew she lived downstairs. She was the biggest Prophet secret yet.

"Nine, come closer," Kerrick said. "I want you to meet the family."

Nine stepped closer to Kerrick who was dressed in an all black suit. "Look around the room. These are your family members." He said softly placing a hand on her shoulder. "This is your uncle Blake and aunt Victory, my son and daughter. They have four children together." He paused. "Noel, Samantha, Isabel and Bethany." They operate the legit portion of our business...The Prophet Estates. A real estate company which owns most of the buildings you'll find in almost every big city around the world."

Nine smiled at all of them. Although they all seemed nice it was Bethany who Nine liked immediately. She held kindness in her eyes and she made her comfortable. And then she remembered something he said. "Grandfather, are you saying that Victory and Blake are..."

"Siblings." He smiled. "Don't worry. Everything I ever did was necessary. To keep the family pure," he said moving on as if it were yesterday's news. "Now this is Marina my daughter and her husband Joshua." He waved toward the other side of the table. "And this is their daughter Alice."

Alice looked upon Nine as if she were seeing a ghost. But Nine smiled and said hello. Everything she did had to be cool. She and Alice would make war, but not at that moment.

"Marina and Joshua run the chain of restaurants we own here on the east coast. They're called *Mama's Kitchen*," he boasted. It felt good that he was able to buy the establishment that once fired him when he was a young man on the come up.

"Finally this is my son Justin and his wife Corrine." Kerrick walked around the table. "And this is Leaf, their son and your cousin. He is the one whose life you saved when you murdered the intruders."

Nine felt as if she had been gut punched. How could she be in love with her cousin? The feelings they had for one another were too strong. It couldn't be possible. Nine's stomach swirled and her head began to bang as she realized what they shared was over.

Leaf was as equally confused since he had just been given the information moments earlier.

"Since we got that out of the way have a seat. It's time to eat," Kerrick said pointing to a chair to the left of him.

Nine walked toward the seat with her head hung low. No wonder so much secrecy surrounded her family. Without even asking Kerrick she knew that her mother and father were probably sister and brother too.

She pulled the seat out and it made a loud screeching noise and she immediately looked at her grandfather. The last thing she wanted was to irritate him before the day started.

Once she was seated she slowly turned her head toward Kerrick. She couldn't stop looking at him. He was the same man who hit her repeatedly with whips for stealing food, tearing into the flesh of her skin. Her nervousness was not only warranted but understandable.

"Eat," Kerrick said to Nine. "It's okay."

Although she wanted to tear into her food, she activated restraint. She took her time forking through the turkey before scooping the mashed potatoes slowly thereafter. She was in no rush. Everything she did had to be deliberate. Like Fran had taught her.

Nine wasn't the only one nervous. Kerrick couldn't stop himself from staring at her. She was beyond intriguing. He kept readjusting his shoulders and Victoria took notice at her husband's change in disposition. He never acted so childishly but there he was, as goofy as a teenage boy.

As Nine ate, Alice and Leaf stared her down. Each having a reason for finding her so interesting.

A few minutes later Kerrick cleared his throat and asked, "How did you learn to…to kill?"

Nine placed the fork down, wiped the corners of her mouth and cleared her throat. She hadn't expected the question. "I never realized I knew how to kill, until I was forced to protect my family." She looked over at Leaf. "If needed I'll do it again."

Kerrick caught the stare between them and was consumed with jealousy. "It's nice that you wanted to protect your cousin. I hate to think what would have happened if they were successful in their attempt."

Nine's heart cracked deeper after reliving the fact that Leaf was blood. It didn't change how she felt. She doubted it ever would. The realization got to Leaf too because he hopped up from the table and rushed out.

When Leaf left Kerrick focused on Nine. "When he comes back I'm going to have him take you to the store. He will buy you some clothing and get you some shoes. I will have my men follow you, but I believe you'll be safe. Gates just made an unsuccessful attempt on Leaf so I doubt if he tries again this soon. Besides, if you're going to dine with kings you must dress for the occasion."

Nine's body was tense as she rode in Leaf's truck on the way to the shopping mall. All of her senses were heightened and she shivered from sensory overload. Driving was a new experience for her. She glanced over at Leaf a few times, and wondered how something so terrifying for her didn't faze him.

"So what do we do now?" he asked as he placed a hand on her thigh.

"About what?"

"Us."

As her mind focused on him as opposed to the car ride it wasn't as bad. "I don't know. I mean, did you know we were related before now?"

He frowned and removed his hand. "Why would you ask me some shit like that? Huh?"

She shrugged. "I'm just trying to find out what's going on. That's all."

He sighed. "Sorry I came at you like that. This is fucking my head up. My parents told me earlier today. They said the fact that most of our aunts and uncles were fucking was why my dad bounced. Said he hadn't spoken to his father until I needed help." He paused. "I'm still confused I guess."

When they finally made it to the mall Leaf walked around to the passenger side of his truck and tried to help her out but she wouldn't move. The cars rolling back and forth and the strange people all made her heart pump.

Frustrated Leaf gripped her head into his hands and looked into her eyes. "I don't know why that nigga kept you under the house but this is me. I'm here with you and there's no reason to be afraid. If you want a chance to start over you have to get out this truck. You not in the basement no more, Nine. You a Prophet. So act like one." He squeezed her face a little harder and then released. He stepped back from the truck. "Are you coming with me or not? The life you want starts here."

Nine thought about everything she'd been through. The beatings. The sessions when Alice would come in and ridicule her for shits and giggles. She realized she was no longer interested in playing the martyr.

So she pushed herself out of the truck. The first step caused her legs to wiggle and she was so terrified she considered running back inside the Escalade and taking cover. But when she got her bearings together she placed both feet on the ground and she looked around. If she wanted to take over the world he was right, now was the time.

So she exhaled and took one step. But when she took her second she knew no one was putting her away anymore. From here on out, she would be free.

CHAPTER TWENTY-EIGHT
NINE

"God save the King! Will no man say, amen?"
-William Shakespeare

Nine looked at herself once more in the new mirror Kerrick had bought for her bedroom. It sat on the door and she didn't recognize herself through its reflection. Her soft curly hair had been stretched into longer flowing curls and she had just a hint of blush on her chocolate skin. She was stunning. She felt confident. And she was learning power.

The dark pink Christian Dior dress hugged her curves and her black bra and panty set kept everything in place. She ran her hands from the outside of her breasts to her hips. "Who are you?" she said to herself. "And what sort of damage will you cause this family?"

Nine pinched herself several times and spun around in the mirror again. Would this be her new life? She wanted to fall in love with it but she also knew her grandfather was a fickle man. His moods changed like the days on a calendar. Each different from the next. But she knew if she wanted to survive she had to face it all.

Nine sat on the edge of her bed to slide on the beautiful black designer shoes he bought her. Leaf picked out everything.

As she slipped on the first, followed by the second she thought about Fran. It was very normal. Fran infiltrated her thoughts and would be the reason behind everything she did.

How she wished she could share this time with her. She envisioned them sharing dinner in the big house and laughing about how at one point in her life she was the weird girl locked in the basement of the Prophet mansion.

Nine would never forget Fran. She would never allow herself to eliminate the lessons she taught her about life. And when the time was right…and only when the time was right…she would avenge her death.

Nine took one more breath and crept up the stairs leading to the rest of the house. She could smell the scent of steak roasting in the oven along with the sweet smell of apple pie. Ever since Nine had murdered the intruders Kerrick hosted several parties to announce her. At one point she was a dirty secret and now he wanted the world to know her. She was a Prophet star.

When she bent the corner Kerrick was holding a glass of wine and speaking to her grandmother Victoria. Leaf was also there with a few other people Nine didn't know. But she did know Alice, who stared at her with malice.

When Kerrick saw Nine standing in front of him his eyes grew as large as the planet Earth. The outfit Leaf selected at the mall was appealing, yet innocent in the same breath. Leaf's selection was a clear indication of how he viewed Nine. He was as captivated with her as was his grandfather.

Kerrick reached out his hand and Nine gravitated toward it as if magnetized. Her tiny brown fingers rested into his palm as he introduced her to the most trusted underbosses. The men who ran the operation that kept the Prophet family filthy rich.

Although the goons met her and acted as if nothing was off they all had questions. How was she a Prophet when she looked nothing like the others? Her complexion was chocolate. It didn't match the others at all. But her beauty screamed I have a right to be here.

When Nine was finally brought to Alice the scowl on her face expressed how she felt. Why was grandfather courting her so much? She was supposed to be nothing more than a toy used for her pleasure. Alice was the favorite! Not Nine!

To Alice's right was her fiancé Hector. His eyes bulged as he looked upon Nine with both fear and lust. Would she speak of the evil things they did to her when the liquor and cocaine forced their hormones out of control?

When she extended her hand to meet Hector they both had their answer. Their secret was safe. "It's a pleasure to meet you," Nine said with a smile so brilliant it could only be perceived as authentic.

Alice tried to control her body but it was difficult and as a result she was shivering. The fact that Nine hadn't cried bloody torture recently meant she was in control of her emotions and that made her deadlier.

After Nine greeted her evil cousin she floated toward the rest of the Prophet gangsters. It was important to meet them all because she was positive she would rule them.

As she spoke everyone wondered where she'd been schooled. Her language both elegant and gangster allowed her to switch back and forth based on the topic or the goon. Versed. Poised. Charming and seductive could all be used to describe her.

Gushing with pride, when she met everyone Kerrick pulled her to a tinier room off of the living room. It was decorated in expensive gold trimmed furniture that was so comfortable you would have to fight not to take a nap.

Nine entered, unaware that her grandfather was admiring her fiercely from behind. Everything about Nine was controlled. The way she operated her legs, the way her arms swayed by her side and how her eyes would consider you for a moment and then leave you in the next, causing you to want to do something interesting to be looked upon once more.

Kerrick was captivated.

Was Nine his beautiful wife coming back to haunt him like she promised on the last day he saw her? Coming back to condemn him for all of the evil, which caused her horrible death?

The questions were many but he had no answers. What he did know was this. If she were there to take him to hell, he would gladly go with her.

Nine took a moment to observe the pictures in the room. They were of all of her family members, even her sisters Lydia and Paige who she never met. Although they were different complexions, and Paige was heavy set, she marveled at how much she looked like her older sister and she wondered where she went. She focused on the gold necklace she was wearing and thought it was beautiful. Did her mother and father buy her the pretty piece?

Finally she settled on something that took her breath away. It sat on the wall boldly as if it were more important than the other photos. "Who is this, grandfather?" she asked as she approached a picture of a woman whose skin was so chocolate she wondered if it were sweet. She turned around and looked at him desiring an answer. "She looks like"— she focused on the picture again— "me."

She was right. The woman did favor her greatly which was part of the reason his heart was captivated by her. "Her name is Thandi and she was my first wife."

Nine observed her again. "She…is beautiful."

He smiled and watered the plants he kept in the room. His love for plants had never changed to keep his hands busy. They were the only things in life that would die without his attention and for that he loved them.

"In the small village where I was born men fought for her. They wanted just one ounce of her attention," he boasted. "But she gave it all to me until her dying day." He put the watering pot down and slid his hands in his pocket.

"How did she die?"

For the first time in days he frowned at her. He was displeased. "Those are things I don't speak about."

Realizing her youth had allowed her to make a wrong move and make him upset it was time to clean up her mess. She was playing chess not checkers. Nine spun around and looked at him. "I would have chosen you too, grandfather."

Kerrick's heart beat skipped before going back to normal. "Why do you talk about things you don't know?"

She glided toward him, her eyes never leaving his. Nine moved as if she were prepared to kiss him and he would have gladly allowed her if she had. Instead she placed her head on his chest and listened to his heartbeat. "In my world, grandfather, you will always be king. There will be no other."

That was all he needed to hear. He needed to know that she would always look upon him with admiration and love, above any man, even Leaf. From that point on Nine would have anything or anybody she wanted. No questions asked.

Suddenly Nine Prophet had become his new favorite. Perhaps she always was. But now the world would know.

Two weeks later Nine was sitting at the dining room table watching the movers bring in elaborate furniture pieces and sculptures to her bedroom. Earlier in the week the walls had been knocked down in the basement to build Nine a fortress fitting of a queen. After the walls were demolished the painters came in and brightened the place. Everything went from gray to vibrant white in an instant. It looked alive.

Now that Nine knew that Kerrick saw his first wife when he saw her face it was important that she played upon it. She seduced him to the point of obsession, causing him to dress better, wear expensive cologne and refrain from bleaching his skin. When Nine asked for anything, she got it. Point, blank, period.

Nine was careful when she tested whether or not Kerrick was under her control. When she wanted new furniture she didn't say, "Grandfather, can you buy me a new bookcase?" She said, "I love our visits, grandfather. And I would feel much better if my place was as handsome as you are when you come see me. I'm ashamed when you come because I feel like it is unworthy of your presence, King."

The next day three designers were sitting in front of Nine with books in hand asking her a million questions to get the basement to be what she envisioned, a castle that resembled one of the pictures in her Cleopatra books, who was one of her idols. Nine had not only learned seduction, she mastered it.

Kerrick's biggest gift was a spectacular bookcase, which stored all of her many novels. It was magnificent and Nine almost cried when she looked upon it.

But there was one major problem with the relationship she was building with her grandfather. He had forbid her from spending time with Leaf. Meetings when the family were together, were the only times she got to see his face and it broke her heart. Because despite the announcement of their kinship both of them had fallen in love.

With the parties out of the way it was now time to discuss business. As Nine sat at the head of the table with Kerrick on the far end, she looked around at her relatives. Alice, her uncle Blake and her cousin Noel were present. Kerrick's loyal goons Riley, Mox and Jameson were also in the building. And of course Leaf was present.

They stole glances at one another and Nine's body felt aroused.

The Prophet family was discussing what could no longer go unaddressed. The fact that Gates had made a move on Kerrick's family member in his home. The penalty was death.

Although Nine had not been given an official seat in his council, the murders she committed on the perpetrators who almost killed Leaf gave her a right to sit at the table. Also whenever possible Kerrick loved looking at her.

"We can't just go into his house and pull him out," Noel said stating the obvious. "We have to be smart, grandfather."

"And I'm not smart?" he yelled.

"I would never disrespect you in that way," he admitted. "You're the most brilliant man I know. It's just that the plan you presented is flawed."

"So if that is the case give me another one," Kerrick demanded as he looked around at his council. "Because right now every plan I raise is being shot down and not replaced with another."

Frustrated with the lack of war planning Nine thought it was best to speak. "I have a plan," she said in a voice so regal they looked around to see who spoke.

Kerrick smiled proudly. "I'm listening."

"Why should she be allowed to say anything?" Alice interrupted, changing the mood abruptly. "She knows nothing about war. Or what it means to be a part of this family. Maybe she should continue to order things to fix her little apartment downstairs instead of dabbling in matters like this."

"That may be true," Nine responded calmly. "I may need more schooling in military art. So teach me my dear cousin. Teach me about war. So that I may learn from the best." Although Nine was being sarcastic it sounded as if she were really soliciting her cousins' help to the others.

Alice remained tight-lipped unable to handle the wits of her cousin.

"I judge by your silence that you are also at a loss," Nine continued. "Perhaps we can learn together."

Alice rolled her eyes and stormed out of the meeting and the house.

Nine grinned inside but appeared confused to everyone else. "Grandfather, I'm sorry. I didn't mean to upset, Alice."

"Don't worry," he said waving her off. "I'm far more interested in this plan of yours. And if we can put it into action. What is it?"

She smiled and exhaled. "I'm wondering if you good men have ever heard the story of the Trojan Horse?"

Silence.

“If not I would be honored if you allow me to tell you a tale.”

CHAPTER TWENTY-NINE

NINE

"You lie in your throat."
-William Shakespeare

Nine was sitting in Leaf's Escalade at a park, miles away from the Prophet mansion. It was a dangerous meeting but they were willing to die for a moment of privacy. Kerrick did all he could to keep them separated and his plan had failed.

Nine looked over at him, wanting to ignore what her heart was feeling. What the world said was eternally wrong. Blood relatives weren't allowed to fall in love. And yet the damage had already been done.

"I love you," Leaf said softly. The moonlight shining in the window bounced against her skin. "I know it's wrong but I can't help it."

Nine looked down at the diamond bracelet her grandfather had given her yesterday. It was magnificent. "He won't let me love you." She looked into his eyes. "Never."

"And you gonna stand for that?" he asked.

The way his eyes sparkled with an ounce of evil had her intrigued. "What are you saying? If you have a plan don't hold it back. Tell me. Let me see if it's worth activating."

"He is going to die, Nine," he said softly. "You and I both know it."

Nine hid the smile that wanted to stimulate her face. She already had a plan to eliminate her grandfather that she told no one. She needed to be sure she could trust him. "He's sick?" Nine asked with raised eyebrows. "I didn't know."

Leaf frowned. "It's amazing. In social environments you are always the brightest in the room. Yet with me you always choose to play dumb." He gripped her wrist, removed the bracelet and tossed it to the floor of his truck. "Maybe you can be real now. Stop fucking around. Be the queen I see in you."

Nine laughed. She had been caught. "Okay," she smiled. "I know what you mean when you say he's going to die. I've always known he must go but everything has a season."

Leaf felt relieved that at least she was prepared to be real with him. "So what's your plan? I know you have one."

"I haven't worked things out fully," she lied. "I just know his days are numbered."

"I don't think for one moment that despite the gifts and the decorations in your apartment downstairs, that you have forgotten about what he's done to you all of your life. What's your plan? I know you want revenge."

"And I will have it."

"Then why move slow?"

Nine's skin was hot to the touch and she wanted to scream but she could hear Fran's voice in her mind. She didn't want to act using her emotions. "Do you know why most criminals get caught?"

"Why?"

"They rush," she said plainly.

"Meaning?"

She looked out ahead of her at the beautiful water sparkling under the moonlight. "I have lived my entire life in terror. I have had people beat me for the fun of it, some who share my same blood and break bread at the table with me in the mansion currently. I have been starved for weeks at a time and forgotten about longer than I care to admit. Yet I'm sitting here, looking at the water with you, with a $50,000 bracelet that belongs to me resting at my feet. And you think the fact that I have restrained myself means I'm slow?" she paused. "A lesser man would've reached across the table and snatched that monster's throat a long time ago, only to be given jail time. But I want it all, so I will stroke him until he turns his back and for that I will be King."

He remained silent.

"When I finally make my move it will be with precision, Leaf," she continued. "And not one thing that happens to him will ever be traced back to me. All I'm doing is preparing to take my throne." She touched his hand. "My next question is will you help me?"

When Nine opened the door leading to her plush apartment in the basement she was met with a basket of smoke. She coughed and screamed. "Fire, fire! Help me!"

Victoria rushed down the stairs but where was Kerrick? She didn't know but the fire department was called and the fire was quickly washed out. Had she not found the fire when she did the entire Prophet mansion would've gone up in flames.

After the men did their job, Nine was allowed downstairs to access the damage. Everything was wet and ruined. The furniture Kerrick bought her and the clothes she had grown to love were all destroyed.

But through it all, the part that hurt the most was that her books were demolished. She picked up the only surviving copy of Shakespeare, that Fran purchased for her years ago which sat in the middle of the floor. For the first time in a long time she dropped to her knees and wept. She wondered who did it. Who could be so cruel? Did Kerrick know about her secret visit and decide to stomp on her heart?

When Nine considered the book again she realized it was unscathed. She looked around the dripping smoke covered interior and wondered why the book was not burnt. Everything else was gone. Was it placed here after the fact? When she opened the thick leather cover she saw Alice's name written in yellow chalk.

Now Nine understood.

Shots were fired.

And now they had their war.

CHAPTER THIRTY
LEAF

"As cold as any stone."
-William Shakespeare

Leaf walked down the long hallway leading to Nine's new room. With the basement burned she was upstairs, closer to Kerrick as he preferred. Leaf wondered if the fire was his doing. Nine kept saying she was clueless on who would be so horrible and Leaf was left to his own thoughts.

He knocked once and walked inside. Nine was sitting in front of a pearl colored vanity brushing her hair. She looked at his reflection through her mirror and smiled. "You know you're being rude right? By not waiting for me to give you permission to enter."

He stood behind her. "You know there aren't any secrets in this house. So why knock? All will be revealed anyway."

She smiled. "What do you want, cousin?"

"You."

Silence.

"I guess you aren't being tactful anymore huh? You know grandfather is right down the hall and yet you tempt his anger anyway."

"There's no need for tact. I know who we are to one another and how I feel about you. I need to know right now if I'm alone in this."

She turned around and looked up at him. "We talked about this in the car at the park," she whispered. "You said you wanted to be with me and I said I needed time. Allow me that and you won't regret it."

"Your nonchalant attitude kills me."

"Then why do you still want me?"

"Because there is no one else. There has never been another person I loved more than you. I tried to walk away, Nine. But in the end I always come back."

"But he will kill you if you express it now, Leaf," she said, allowing her emotion to spill slightly.

"Then let there be blood." She stood up and walked toward him. He wrapped his arms around her and held onto her tightly. "You have to be careful, Nine. My father is working closely with Kerrick to pay off the debt my actions have caused. In a few meetings some of the family members have been talking about you. They're saying how they hate that Kerrick has taken a liking to you, and that you are in a position to get it all. I don't know what their intentions are but it sounds dangerous."

She raised her head and asked, "You think he'll let them touch me?"

"He may lead the pack. Especially if he doesn't get what he wants."

She pulled away from him and sat on the edge of the bed. "And what's that?"

"Sex."

She laughed. "Sex is a weapon in war, cousin. Sometimes, it's a necessary evil."

CHAPTER THIRTY-ONE
THE PROPHET FAMILY

"O God of battles. Steel my soldiers' hearts."
-William Shakespeare

Gates slid up to the alarm panel by his front door an activated the top-notch system in his mansion. When he was done he walked to the control room and viewed all of the monitors. From his vantage point he could see it all. Everything was peaceful outside of his compound and he was prepared to get some sleep.

There was one problem; Gates was so busy keeping the elements out of his house that he never considered the problem was already inside.

Weeks back when Nine thought of a proposal to kill Gates, her plan was not to attack his property from the outside. She suggested striking from the inside using slow and precise methods.

She told them about the Trojan Horse tale. The Trojan Horse was assumed to be a trophy gift to the Troy Army from the Greeks after a recent victory on Troy's part. The large wooden horse, which secretly housed a Greek Army, was proudly pushed into Troy. Troy wanted to show the city how they beat the army. Under the cover of night the Greek Army burst out of the Trojan Horse and attacked their enemy from the inside. They defeated Troy and destroyed the beautiful city.

So three days ago, Leaf and eight of Nine's cousins set up camp in a large landscaping truck outside of the Gates Compound. Kerrick paid one of the trusted men allowed to enter Gates' property to tend to his landscape. Every day for eight days this trusted man would bring a new member with him to work. But what Gates didn't realize was that although two men would enter, only the trusted man would leave.

Once inside they set up shop in his unfinished basement and went over the plan of attack. They could've killed Gates by himself a long time ago but that wasn't the plan. Kerrick wanted him alive so he could live with his loss.

Instead, the Prophet army plotted. They ate the food they brought with them and when it was time they moved out of the basement and into the house.

When Gates eased under the covers to spoon his wife, he was startled when he felt leather gloves. He jumped out of bed preparing to grab his gun but it had already been taken.

The man in the bed was Leaf and he rolled out of bed and removed his mask. He wanted to come personally since Gates had done all he could to kill him. "You should've taken Kerrick's money, instead of trying to take my life."

Gates shook his head and tried to remain calm. It was beyond difficult since he had no idea where his wife and thirteen year old twin girls were. "What do you want?" he asked no longer as powerful as he usually was. "I have money downstairs."

Leaf removed the phone from his pocket. "We already have it. But the first thing you're going to do is tell my grandfather which one of your daughters you choose to remain alive."

Gate's body trembled and he erupted into a quiet cry. Choosing between his daughters was not only impossible; it was the worst thing he could imagine. "Please don't," he sobbed. "They are innocent."

"Nobody is innocent in war. Remember? You came into the Prophet mansion and tried to kill me. The difference is I'm still here."

"But you murdered my daughter and—"

"She got mad and pulled a gun on me because I fucked her and left her," he interrupted. "That was my only crime. I'm a kid. If you mad about that you charge it to the game, not my life." He tossed Gates the phone and he caught it. "Talk to Kerrick. Tell him which daughter to keep alive or he will kill them both."

Gates placed the phone against his ear and sobbed. He would've preferred a thousand deaths than to choose between one of his children.

Without even saying hello Kerrick said, "Which one?" Gates could hear his wife and his twin girls weeping in the background.

"Please don't do this," Gates begged. "I'm begging you."

"Time is of the essence and I'm a man of my word."

Realizing Kerrick was unrelenting, Gates went deep into his mind and recalled past memories about Dymond and Berry Gates. Dymond woke up every morning with something positive to say about her life, while Berry took to analyzing the world and the things around her. She trusted no one.

When he was done with that thought he considered their appearances. Dymond always took an extra minute to make sure her hair was perfect and her makeup was in place. Berry preferred zero makeup while throwing her hair into wild ponytails. She felt beauty was a waste of time.

When he finished making the decision best for himself he placed his lips to the phone and said, "I choose Berry to remain alive."

"Done."

A machine gun let off in the background and Dymond's life was snuffed out instantly. Gates cried to the Gods because the pain in his chest ripped at him. The only thing he had to look forward to would be dying soon so that he could be with his naive princess.

But death would not come to him soon enough.

When the work was done The Prophet family packed up. "We have already emptied your stash houses in Baltimore," Leaf said to Gates. "We aren't foolish enough to believe that what we collected was all the money or product you owned. But for now it will be good." He paused. "Now someone will be in contact with you soon to negotiate the business that you pushed back from for so many years with Kerrick. Considering everything going on he thinks you will make great business partners. I do too."

"What if I don't work with him?" he yelled, emboldened by the promise to keep him alive.

Leaf pulled out a list of names and addresses. He handed them to him. "You can keep that copy. We have others."

Gates briefly scanned over the document. He knew exactly what it was. The addresses of everyone he loved. His wife's parents, his only living aunts, uncles, everybody he cared about was on that paper. And that included friends.

"We don't want anymore war, Gates," Leaf said. "Your remaining daughter and wife will be let go and returned to you. We realize that you are a made man. So let the violence stop here. Because if you don't, our next move will be final for everyone you know and love."

CHAPTER THIRTY-TWO

NINE

ONE MONTH LATER

"Could I come near your beauty with my nails, I'd set my ten commandments in your face."
-William Shakespeare

Today was the best information in seventeen year old Nine's life. She had gotten news from her relatives that her grandfather was dying. Although she still met with the Prophet army, in an effort to know all of the ends and outs, she played the vigilant granddaughter.

She was also expecting a child of her own. Lord Knight Prophet was due in eight months and she couldn't be happier. Although life had gotten better after the plan to take Gates down was successful, even on his dying bed Kerrick's lust grew each day.

He would no longer accept her brush off. If she wanted the kingdom she had to first render to the sitting king.

A week after the successful plan she created to infiltrate the Gates' mansion Kerrick was consumed with lust. And he was no longer interested in denying his thirsts.

It was midnight when Kerrick knocked softly on his granddaughter's door. He was carrying a small bag.

"Come in, grandfather," she said softly.

He placed his hand on the cool knob and turned it slowly. Before entering he looked down the hall for his wife. It wasn't as if he wasn't allowed to do what he pleased anyway, he just didn't want any interruptions.

Once inside of the room he stared at his granddaughter. The bulge from her growing baby was not big enough yet to give away her and Leaf's secret. She was draped in a silk green nightie that brushed against her hips, exposing most of her lower body. She turned around and walked toward her vanity mirror. Now he could see her red thong before it disappeared into the flesh of her cheeks. She sat down at her vanity and brushed her hair.

Excited, he locked the door and strolled up to her.

Before he gave her the gift she asked, "Do you think we're monsters, grandfather?" her mood was as calm as her brush strokes, deliberate but precise.

"Why do you ask?"

She sat the brush down, turned around in her chair and stood up. Then she allowed the silk nightie she was wearing to float to her ankles. She was now naked, with the exception of her red thong.

Kerrick felt lightheaded when he observed her body. She was more spectacular than he remembered Thandi to be.

"Is that for me, grandfather?" she asked looking at the bag dangling in his hand.

Kerrick swallowed. He had forgotten all about the gift. It wasn't like he didn't see her nudeness many times before. On the contrary he had, every time he took a whip to her flesh in an effort to break her mentally. But this time was different. She was in control, not him and he knew it.

"Yes," he said.

"May I have it?" she asked with a wide smile. "I just love gifts." She extended her hand and the diamond bracelet she wore sparkled. He handed it to her and she removed a red box from the bag. When she opened the lid a necklace draped with five diamonds sat inside. Her eyes widened with excitement. "I love it, grandfather! Can you put it on me?" she turned around and he removed the necklace. In the mirror she saw her naked body as Kerrick standing behind her in utter amazement.

While he clasped the necklace he reviewed the scars he'd added to her body. He ran his hand over the healed ripped flesh and a single tear fell from his eyes. "I never got a chance to say I'm sorry."

"It's okay, grand—"

"Please, let me finish," he said raised his hand cutting her off. "I never shared my story with anyone. I led a difficult life where the more violent you were the greater your chances of surviving. But there were two times I regretted my decisions. The first was when my actions caused my wife to be murdered and the second is this moment. I regret abusing you and I regret the lust I have for you in my heart."

Nine turned around and looked up at him. "I'm a woman now, grandfather. And tonight, I beg you to look at me as your wife. Thandi. Bury your worries inside of me. Soon all will be over."

Her words rocked his core and he led her to the bed. He was slow and meticulous with her body. In his mind he had been given another chance to make love to his wife and he would not waste a minute.

A few days after Kerrick took Nine into her bed he was severely ill and the doctors were certain he would not survive. Believing he was being poisoned because they could not find a cause, they tested his food and drink but everything was clean. Whatever was getting him ill was internal and was not ingested.

Before long he had been given only hours to live. He had already taken a separate room in the mansion, away from his wife, so that he could be alone with thoughts of Nine and Thandi.

As he lie on his deathbed he called Victoria and Nine to his bedside. While he waited on them to enter he watered the beautiful plant that Nine bought him almost two months earlier. It had certainly grown.

When Victoria and Nine finally came into the room, Victoria's face was wet with tears. Nine also acted as if she were inconsolable at her grandfather's condition. "I'm dying," he said plainly. "And there is nothing more they can do for me."

"No," Victoria screamed dropping to her knees. "Please don't leave me."

"Victoria, please," he responded out of breath. He was in no mood for her performances. "I need you to remain calm."

Embarrassed she stood to her feet and held his hand while Nine gripped the other. "The doctor believes I have cancer but because I refuse to go to the hospital he can't be sure. And I'm okay with dying."

"Why don't you just go get help, Kerrick?" she begged. "Please."

"I'm sixty-six years old. And while some may believe that age is young I am tired. My life has been everything I wanted up to this point. I migrated here from Africa as a poor man and then was blessed with a family and more riches than I deserved. It's okay. I have lived the American Dream. And I'm ready to die."

Victoria knew he was hoping to see Thandi in the next life but there was no use in arguing. She could never control him and she wouldn't start today.

Suddenly Alice burst into the room. "Grandfather, I just heard what was happening. Why didn't you call for me?" she responded her face blush red from crying.

"Because I wanted to meet with Victoria and Nine first." He frowned. "Now leave. This is a private conversation. I will call for the rest of the family later."

Alice's jaw hung and her eyes widened. "But I—"

"Alice, don't make me say it again!" he yelled using the little energy he could spare. "Leave at once and I will meet with you later."

Alice looked at Nine but Nine's expression was filled with concern. Nine was great with maintaining her poker face. Someone looking in would think that Nine felt bad that Alice was being treated so badly. But Alice could see beyond the façade and knew that Nine loved every minute of it.

When she left Kerrick said, "I want you to carry out my wishes exactly as I have them outlined, Victoria." He paused. "Nine is to get my home and half of my possessions. You will get the other half."

"Half?" she paused looking at Nine as if she had spoken. "But what about the other children?" she focused back on him. Kerrick had her sign a prenuptial agreement when he was a young broke man. In the agreement he specified that in the event of his death or a divorce, she could possibly walk away with nothing. So she had no say so even as his wife.

"These are my wishes, Victoria. And I've already spoken to my attorney. He has a copy of my will. If you disobey me you will be cut out of everything."

"But why?" she cried and pinched her neck.

"Because I have treated Nine terribly and this is my feeble attempt to make amends. Before I see my maker." He paused. "I have done a lot of things, Victoria. Some things I can never repeat but I will not leave this world without doing right by her. Do you understand? Will you do what I asked?"

Victoria looked up at Nine and then at Kerrick. "You fucked her didn't you?" she yelled. "Must you fuck all of your children?"

Kerrick sighed. She and he both knew that he never touched one of his relatives, before Nine. He also realized based on her attitude that his wife would not do what he wanted. So he got on the phone and contacted his attorney with both of them standing in the room. When the call was over Nine had become the executor over the entire estate. She ruled and would determine how things would be divided.

Victoria was beside herself with anger. "I have loved you all of my young life," she sobbed. "I have given up my body to bare your children. I have given up my morals to follow your rule and I gave you my heart." She placed her hand over her chest. "And this is how you repay me?" When he didn't respond she stormed out leaving them alone. Her performance was certainly theatrical but it didn't change his opinion.

Kerrick reached out his hand and pulled her closer. "Your family will hate you after this but you're strong enough to deal with it. I know it. I hope you have the life that you've dreamed of. The one you dreamed about from your books." He reached over on the table and handed her some keys and four brown leather journals. "The downstairs has been repaired. I want you to go and look what I've done for you. And when you have some time I want you to read about my life. I've depicted it as best as I could in these books. Trust me, it's rough and you will look at me differently." He yawned. "I'm tired now my dear, Nine. I want some rest."

"I love you, grandfather," she said kissing him on his eyelids.

He looked directly into her eyes. "I know that you are responsible for my death. I always knew this day would come. And I'm okay with it now."

Nine was shocked. "I don't understand, grandfather. I didn't do anything."

"This plant you placed at my bedside is known as the grim reaper. You gave it to me to take my life, and I always knew I would die by your hand," he responded before closing his eyes. "There's no need in lying."

Nine was impressed. He could've ousted her a long time ago and he didn't. He was taking his murder like a G.

So she ran out of his room to see what was in store for her. When she used the keys to enter the room she was captivated when she saw the celling to floor cherry bookshelves. Not only did he have them built, he also stocked up the first shelf with Shakespeare, Edgar Allen Poe and other great writers of her time. She was blown away.

"I hope you know this isn't over," Alice said walking up behind her.

At first Nine threw on her innocent mask but her grandfather was dying soon and she would reign supreme. What was the use in being fake?

Nine walked up to her and stared dead into her eyes. "Alice, we will have our day. Very soon. I suggest you get your body ready."

CHAPTER THIRTY-THREE
NINE

"Memory, the warder of the brain."
-William Shakespeare

Kerrick Prophet, born Kerrick Khumalo of Zimbabwe, died on a Tuesday. His ceremony was uneventful. The only members who came were those of the Prophet family and that was mostly because they wanted their faces recorded in case Kerrick had stipulated their presence being required in his will.

The next day, the entire family was summoned to the law office of Bradley Howard for the reading of the will. The family sat in one of the conference rooms while the attorney stood behind a podium in the front. Everyone but Nine and Victoria was surprised when they learned that Nine had been given everything. After the will was read Nine stood up and approached the podium. She looked at Bradley Howard and said, "You can leave now. I would like to address my family."

"Sure," he said rushing out of the room.

When he left she looked upon the Prophet family. She winked at Leaf who stood proudly in the back, while leaning on the wall. "Although I only recently met some of you I don't know you personally. I would like to take this time to introduce myself. My name is Nine Prophet and I was abused by Kerrick for sixteen years of my life. He has left me everything and I will be fair to those who choose to follow my rules. But if you try to sue me for this money you will fail and be given nothing. There are only two exceptions to my generosity. Alice and Victoria will be given nothing."

"But why?" Victoria sobbed.

"Because you allowed my aunts and uncles to be raised in an incestuous environment and did nothing. Because of it my parents were never able to care for me, my life was torture and now I am in love with my cousin."

"But I was a victim too!"

"And they were children. You were their mother and you failed." She paused. "Now you will live the life the only mother I knew led. You will be depressed. You will be broke and you will spend every moment with the realization that you fell in love with the wrong man. Just like my precious Fran. Now leave."

Victoria ran out of the room sobbing.

"I know many of you do not agree with what I just did. But my decision is final. This meeting is adjourned." Alice was about to walk out until Nine said, "Alice, we will have our moment soon. I haven't forgotten."

When Alice woke up she was sitting in a wooden chair with a rag in her mouth. She had been poisoned and abducted in the middle of the night. She was in an abandoned property in Maryland that the Prophet family had just acquired. Her arms were tied behind the chair and her ankles to the legs. Nine stood in front of her dressed in a black cat suit with red boots. Without even speaking, she brought a whip down over Alice's face. The pain was unbearable.

"Hello, Alice," Nine grinned. "Are you ready to reap what you sowed?"

With limited mouth movements Alice said, "Please don't do this. I'm sorry for everything."

"Now, now, my dear, Alice. I never once begged for mercy. Did I? Instead I took what you dished and kept on living. And I must ask that you do the same." She paused. "And just so you know, Hector has been murdered. You are alive because you share my blood-line. But don't make me kill you too."

Nine snapped her fingers and three men appeared from the darkness of the building. They were naked and held the largest penises she had ever seen in her life.

"They are going to do whatever they please with your body for sixteen weeks. Unlike me you will be fed but only when you do what is asked. If you buck the sys-tem you will be kept for an additional week or killed."

Nine looked at one of the naked men. He quickly untied Alice's arms and took off the mouth tie. "Come here, Alice." Alice stood up and Nine said, "You know the rules, Alice." She pointed to the floor. "Always ap-proach me on your knees."

Huge tears rolled down her cheek as she crawled to her cousin. Just like she had done to her.

"Remove my boot," Nine ordered.

Alice obeyed, freeing Nine's foot. "Now lick it clean."

Nine sat in the backseat of a limousine as she prepared to meet Gates. She was taken on a drive, along a road covered with gravel that swept around an S shape curve. When the limo stopped in front of a mansion the door was opened and a handsome gentleman extended his hand to help Nine out. After Gates' young daughter was murdered he moved to a more secure compound.

"Ms. Prophet, Right this way."

Nine placed her hand into his and was led up huge steps leading to a large porch. Large marble columns stood powerfully on each end and the windows sparkled like diamonds. She was led to a door dazzled with gold streaks and into a dining room with comfortable burgundy furniture accented in black wood. A sparkling fire danced and she felt comfortable.

"Mr. Gates will be right with you," the man said before exiting.

Now alone, Nine observed the obscure painting on the wall as she waited to meet her host. It looked like a bleeding vagina. Two minutes later Gates walked up behind her and observed the painting she was admiring.

"It was done by a young artist named Antoinette Bateau. She was a young whore whose head was decapitated by her pimp for leaving him. She fell in love with one of her many johns and he was beside himself with jealousy. So he snuffed her life."

Nine turned around and observed Gates who was standing so closely she had no room to move. She smiled seductively and took a seat. He sat next to her. "Who are you?" he asked as if they hadn't conversed already.

"Nine Prophet," she said coyly. "Have you forgotten me already?"

"How could I? You have done something I have been trying to do for most of my life. Rid the world of Kerrick Prophet. But you are also the scavenger who I saw the night in the kitchen."

"Then if you know me"— she crossed her legs and the black dress she wore slid back revealing her garter belt— "why must you continue to ask?"

"Because I don't know your motive."

"You shouldn't worry about motives, Mr. Gates. They are so troublesome. Just know that I am a woman of my word and I have proven it to you."

"A young woman," he interrupted.

"But a woman all the same."

He grinned. "Can I ask you how you did it? They say he wasn't poisoned. He wasn't shot or stabbed. How did you eliminate the man who killed one of my daughters and changed my life forever?"

"If that story interests you so much I will tell you. But first I need to talk business. My grandfather had been trying to tap into the Baltimore market all of his life. He was not a man of his word but I am. So I'm asking will you partner with me and allow my family to continue to supply your needs?"

"You're so young. Can't be more than seventeen or eighteen if my guess is correct. What do you possibly know about the drug business?"

"I am young but I'm smart. While most girls my age busied themselves with trivial thoughts of boys, clothes and makeup, I sat in a room day after day and was forced to use my mind." She responded. "Yes, Sir Gates. I am young. But I am king. And I have a council who is loyal to me and will tell me everything I need to know."

He shook his head and grinned. If nothing else, doing business with her would be entertaining. "You have a deal."

"What about Leaf Prophet? You still agree to leave him alone?"

He bit his tongue but he knew it was time to let that chapter go in his life. "I agree." He exhaled. "Now please, will you tell me how you killed him?"

Nine stood up and brushed the back of her dress. "My grandfather loved plants. All of his life. So I bought him a beautiful one. It was speckled in purple and white flowers. There was no way he could resist it. But, the plant was also poisonous, and sat next to his bed everyday as he breathed in its fatal fumes. When he finally touched it he was killed."

"What kind of plant was it?"

"An Aconite."

Gates was stunned at her calculating manner but was also turned on. "You are dangerous," he admitted.

"One man's danger is another man's peace."

CHAPTER THIRTY-FOUR

NINE

SOME MONTHS LATER

"Delays have dangerous ends."
-William Shakespeare

Nine eased out of her extra large king bed and waddled toward the window. She pushed the thick brown velvet curtain aside just enough for the sunshine to spill inside. The bright rays temporarily blinded her.

She smiled and rubbed her eight-month-old pregnant belly. Her life was so different and she feared that things would change for the worse. After all, she lived a life frowned upon in society and her heart said her unborn child would pay for her sins.

"You okay?" Leaf asked as he yawned and looked over at his girlfriend.

Nine pressed a button and the curtains pulled back completely back automatically, dousing the room with life.

She strolled toward him and sat on the edge of the bed. She placed her hand on his face and her fingertips brushed against his smooth five o'clock shadow. "I'm happy. That's it and that's all."

"Be real with me, baby. What you thinking about?"

She removed her hand and rubbed her belly. "If I'm being honest I will say that I'm afraid. I wake up everyday worried that we will never get married or be happy. We're cousins and yet we have sex and are in love."

Leaf threw his head back into the fluffy pillows. "Nine, why do we have to go over this every week? When you stayed in the basement you never cared about what others thought. Don't be like grandfather who hated who he was when he migrated from Africa. You free, you different. We are in love and you're carrying my baby. Or are you saying you don't want to marry me?"

Nine's head drooped. "I'm not saying that. It's just that…well.. what if our baby is…deformed?"

"That won't happen."

"But how do you know?"

"Even if it does we will take care of it and love it like we are supposed to, Nine. Are you sure you aren't worried about the beef brewing with the Alvarez Cartel?"

Nine's entire disposition changed. Her shoulders hardened and her eyes lowered. "Have I ever given you any reason to believe that I scare easily?"

"Never."

"Then why would you disrespect me like that?" she walked into the middle of the room. "I am worried about our child, Leaf. If it were different I would've said it. After grandfather died I stopped being scared of anything that breathes. And that includes the Cartel. All I'm asking is that you take me seriously. Please."

Leaf eased out of bed and walked toward Nine. He rubbed her shoulders and kissed her softly. "We are cousins and we are in love. If that's wrong that's the cross you have to bear. But I'm holding it with you. I'm asking you not to forget that." He brushed her face with his hand. "My only question is, are you strong enough to be my wife?"

He pulled her head toward him and his tongue snaked into her mouth. He led her to the bed with a kiss. Nine was lying on the bed on her side with her knees bent for comfort in her condition. He eased her gown over her belly and it draped along the side of her waist. He pushed her leg opened and revealed her pink center. It was glistening like it always was whenever she was aroused.

Turned on, he released himself from his pajama pants, lie on his side behind Nine and pushed into her tightness. Nine moaned and bit down on her bottom lip as he stroked inside of her body softly. "I love you, Nine," he whispered in her ear. "More than anything. I need you to know that."

"And I will die for you."

"You may have to."

Nine was in the car with her cousin Bethany on the way to the mall. Over the months she had become a confidant. Unlike some of the other cousins who only called on Nine when they wanted a larger amount of money deposited into their accounts, than what was already distributed to them each month, Bethany sincerely cared about how Nine was doing. It bothered her that during her many visits to the Prophet mansion she never knew Nine existed.

Bethany was in the passenger seat of Nine's silver Maserati and she was applying blush. She was just as beautiful as the other Prophets but she was also fun loving and honest. "I think you're worried too much about what other people think."

"That's not it, I just don't know about marrying him," Nine admitted. "It just seems so wrong."

Bethany exhaled and put down her brush. "Nine, this is our life. We grew up like this and we don't know anything else. You fell in love with the person who made you smile and he just happens to be your cousin. The only reason you feel some kind of way is because of all of the death threats we've been receiving lately." She shrugged. "I guess that's why grandfather kept it a secret so long."

"Yeah, I don't like people calling us in breeders and shit like that."

"But we are."

"So why is it so bad?" Nine asked seriously.

"You're asking the wrong person."

Nine exhaled. She didn't get the answer she wanted but at the end of the day she knew her cousin was right. As weird as their world was, it was still their world. If she was going to hell she prepared herself to fry. "On another note, have you spoken to Alice?" Nine asked.

"Nope. Ever since you cut her out of the family fortune, nobody has seen or heard from her."

True to Nine's promise she kept Alice in that building for sixteen weeks. She didn't tell a soul. She was raped without condoms and abused and only then was she released.

"Do you think she has anything to do with the threats we've been receiving?" Nine asked.

"Could be the Alvarez Cartel. Or it could be her. She was granddaddy's favorite and to know that she was cut out of the fortune fucks with her head."

Nine considered what Bethany said when a number she didn't recognize appeared on her cell phone. She hit the button of the Bluetooth, which allowed the call to come over the airwaves. "Is this Nine Prophet?" someone asked.

"Yes."

"You need to get down to Baltimore Central Booking right away. Leaf has been arrested."

Nine's heart rate increased. "For what?"

"Transporting cocaine."

CHAPTER THIRTY-FIVE
NINE

"Unbidden guests are often welcomest when they are gone."

-William Shakespeare

Nine was looking at her fiancé through Plexiglas in jail. Her hands were sweaty because she didn't understand what was going on. Not only was he arrested, but his face was also battered. His right eye was huge and black.

What was he even doing in prison? She built her operation so that she and anybody close to her never had to touch drugs. They had mules and other men for those types of jobs. So where did Leaf go wrong?

"I'm telling you, baby," he paused, "I didn't do this shit. I was set up."

"By who?""

"I don't know," he said. "And that's all I can say right now." They realized that anything they said could be used against them in court so the conversation was kept at a minimum.

"So what happened to your face," she asked softly.

"It's nothing," he lied. "I don't want you worrying because you still carrying my baby."

"Leaf, I'm asking you a question. What happened?"

"Somebody said something fucked up about the family. Saying we fuck our own people and shit like that. Like I said I don't want you worrying about those things. I just want you to be careful. Somebody is obviously trying to tear us down and I don't know why."

Nine's face was calm but her mind was racing. Whoever was trying to break her had better come prepared for the fight. Because she had intentions on battling to the death.

Nine just returned home after a long day. First she saw an attorney to get Leaf out of jail but he admitted that it would be easier said than done. Besides, Leaf was caught with bricks of cocaine with a street value of 1.3 million dollars. By all accounts he was federally fucked.

After taking a shower she decided to take a nap before doing some more research on what it would take to get him released. She had already met with members of the Prophet family about her drug operation and they had tightened security.

Exhausted, she drew the blinds so that her room was pitch black, the way she liked it. Like it was when she lived in the basement. She was in bed and her eyes were closed for one minute before a sheet was placed over her head. Suddenly she was struck repeatedly about the face and belly with a blunt object. Nine tried to fight but she was no match for whoever was trying to kill her.

When the blows slowed, the sheet was ripped off of her face and for a second she saw the glimpse of a tiny gold butterfly pendent moments before a pillow was pressed over her head. Her assailant was a woman.

This gave Nine the few spurts of energy she needed to fight harder but it was in vain. She had suddenly become lightheaded and before she knew it she blacked out.

When the beating was over Nine was lying on her side, on the marble floor in her bedroom. She was covered in blood and she felt something lodged between the middle of her legs. When she moved her hand to feel what was there, she felt the head of her baby.

Terrified Nine crawled to the phone on the dresser because she was unable to walk. With the little stamina she had left, she raised her hand, knocked the phone off of her dresser and called 911.

CHAPTER THIRTY-SIX

PRESENT DAY

WINTER, BALTIMORE, MD

PENN STATION

"Fight till the last gasp."
-William Shakespeare

The train rocked as it sped down the track on the way to North Carolina. Six months ago Nine lost her baby and after some investigation Nine had found her perpetrator. Butterfly sat across the table from Nine clutching her own baby on the train. Bulky tears cruised down her face and rolled to her neck.

The Predator gazed out of the window at the acres of greenery. "It's beautiful isn't it?" she said. "It really showcases God's grace." Slowly she turned and eyed Butterfly.

"So there's nothing I can say to convince you to let me go," she twittered. "All I want to do is be with my baby, Nine. That's all I've ever wanted."

"I'm afraid that's not possible," the Predator smiled. "The road for you ends here." She seemed self-possessed and this frightened Butterfly even more. "I always wanted to know this question. Why did you try to kill me? You were my sister, Paige. I had no beef with you, I've never met you. Here you sit asking me to let you keep your child yet you took the life of mine."

Paige, also known as Butterfly, bottom lip trembled. "I'll tell you but first I have to know. How did you know it was me?"

"The butterfly necklace you're wearing. I saw it in a picture in the sitting room at the Prophet mansion."

"A picture of me?" she laughed. "Kerrick never spoke to me or my sister. Why would he have a picture?"

"It was there. I remember clearly looking at the necklace and wanting one for myself. I always wondered where you were sister. I always wondered if you were okay but I never imagined that you would try to kill me. Why, Paige? I would've thought Alice would do something like this not you."

Butterfly sighed. "I did it because you had it all!" she yelled.

Nine looked at her as if she were someone new. "Had it all?" she repeated. "I was tortured, raped and humiliated for sixteen years of my life. How could I have it all?"

"You were tortured but at least someone touched you," she responded. "I would've given the world to be abused just to be seen. No one saw me, Nine. Ever! And when Lydia died I lost the only other person who cared."

"So you blamed me for that?"

"I despised that you had mother's love."

"Mother's love? She didn't speak to me. Ever!"

"You're foolish," Butterfly laughed. "You think she didn't love you just because she didn't talk to you?

Don't you realize that she gave up the little life she had with grandfather to save yours? She loved you the only way she knew how. By sacrifice. Which is more than I can say she did for me."

"But where were you? I was told you ran away, but how did you survive?" the Predator asked.

"I wandered down the road distraught and some neighbors took me in. I never spoke of or mentioned my family and after awhile they were able to adopt me. But it doesn't take away how much I wanted mothers love." Butterfly said.

Nine's mind felt cluttered. There were so many questions and so little time. "Did you have anything to do with the cocaine that was placed into Leaf's car? Because he would've still been in jail if it wasn't for our attorney."

"No," she answered truthfully. "That probably was Alice."

Nine exhaled. She had to find that bitch before she struck again. Remembering the present The Predator said, "My life will never be the same because of you. Ever."

"And I'm sorry," Butterfly replied. "I truly am." Realizing all was lost she lowered her head and brushed the sleeping baby's face with her index finger. "I never thought we'd have this short of a time together," she whispered to her son. "My mistakes," her voice choked, "your mama's mistakes have brought us to this end. And I'm so sorry." When she was done talking to her baby she looked at the Predator and said, "I'm ready."

"Okay," she smiled eerily. The Predator took in the view again. "Look, Butterfly. Look out of the window at the land. Isn't it spectacular?"

Butterfly's jaw trembled. Her face reddened as she slowly turned her head. Her eyes landed on the sun. It was rising and was brilliantly orange. Just at that moment a group of yellow butterflies fluttered in front of the window. Were they a figment of her imagination, or were angels preparing to take her to a better place. None of it mattered because a gun, with a silencer attached, was placed against the back of her head and her brains were blown out.

The soldier looked upon the Predator and waited for his next order. "The baby?" he asked.

"Hand him to me," she responded.

He tucked his weapon in his leather gun belt and lifted the child out of his deceased mothers arms. He handed the baby, who was now awake, to Nine. His face was speckled with drops of his mother's blood and they resembled freckles.

"It's so sad," The predator said in an artificial tone. "I want so badly to let you live but I know if I do, you will eventually kill me for revenge. So I have to do what I must."

She raised her hand and placed it over the child's face. She pressed her palm down not needing a lot of energy to kill an infant. At first the child's arms fluttered but after awhile it stopped moving. She was more like Kerrick than she realized.

She raised her hand and the baby's eyes were closed. She stood up and placed the child back into his mother's arms. Just at that moment the train stopped and she prepared to walk out with her goons until there was a noise.

She turned around and saw that the baby had survived after all. His eyes were open and his legs jerked before he cried loudly.

Nine couldn't help but smile. He was a fighter like her. "That's it, baby. Fight 'till the last gasp," she said quoting Shakespeare.

The infant reminded her of herself and she would not leave him. Could not leave him. Instead she decided to raise him as her own and mention nothing, ever, to him about his mother.

Cradling the baby in her arms she looked down at his perfect face and walked toward he exit. "And I will raise you as a God."

RICH BITCH

The Pussy MOB

A NOVEL BY

CHANEL MURPHY

RICH BITCH

THE MEANEST OF THEM ALL

A NOVEL BY

TIFFANI MURPHY

A SCHOOL OF Dolls

A NOVEL

PAIGE LOHAN

The Cartel Collection
Established in January 2008
We're growing stronger by the month!!!
www.thecartelpublications.com

Cartel Publications Order Form
Inmates ONLY get novels for $10.00 per book!

Titles		*Fee*
Shyt List		$15.00
Shyt List 2		$15.00
Pitbulls In A Skirt		$15.00
Pitbulls In A Skirt 2		$15.00
Pitbulls In A Skirt 3		$15.00
Pitbulls In A Skirt 4		$15.00
Victoria's Secret		$15.00
Poison		$15.00
Poison 2		$15.00
Hell Razor Honeys		$15.00
Hell Razor Honeys 2		$15.00
A Hustler's Son 2		$15.00
Black And Ugly As Ever		$15.00
Year of The Crack Mom		$15.00
The Face That Launched a Thousand Bullets		$15.00
The Unusual Suspects		$15.00
Miss Wayne & The Queens of DC		$15.00
Year of The Crack Mom		$15.00
Paid in Blood		$15.00
Shyt List III		$15.00
Shyt List **IV**		$15.00
Raunchy		$15.00
Raunchy 2		$15.00
Raunchy 3		$15.00
Jealous Hearted		$15.00
Quita's Dayscare Center		$15.00
Quita's Dayscare Center 2		$15.00
Shyt List V		$15.00
Deadheads		$15.00
Pretty Kings		$15.00
Pretty Kings II		$15.00
Drunk & Hot Girls		$15.00
Hersband Material		$15.00
Upscale Kittens		$15.00
Wake & Bake Boys		$15.00
Young & Dumb		$15.00
Tranny 911		$15.00
Tranny 911: Dixie's Rise		$15.00
First Comes Love Then Comes Murder		$15.00
Young & Dumb: Vyce's Getback		$15.00
Luxury Tax		$15.00
Mad Maxxx		$15.00
The Lying King		$15.00
Crazy Kind of Love		$15.00
Silence of the Nine		$15.00

Please add $4.00 per book for shipping and handling.
The Cartel Publications * P.O. Box 486 * Owings Mills * MD * 21117

Name: ____________________

Address: ____________________

City/State: ____________________

Contact # & Email: ____________________

Please allow 5-7 business days for delivery. The Cartel is not responsible for prison orders rejected.

Personal Checks Are Not Accepted.

Made in the USA
Lexington, KY
20 March 2015